TIME DONE BEEN
WON'T BE NO MORE

ALSO BY WILLIAM GAY

TIME DONE BEEN
WON'T BE NO MORE

–Collected Prose–

by William Gay

———

Wild Dog Press
Brush Creek, TN

Wild Dog Press
91 Vantrease Rd
Brush Creek, TN 38547
michaelwhite@dtccom.net

Gay, William
Time Done Been Won't Be No More: Collected Prose

ISBN   978-0-9765202-5-2

Cover painting by William Gay
Compiled and edited by J. M. White
Jacket design by John Cipollina
Book design by Lamont Ingalls
Author photo by Greg Hobson

Contents

ILLUSTRATIONS

SHORT STORIES

Time Done Been Won't Be No More

COME HOME, COME HOME, IT'S SUPPERTIME

HIS DREAMS WERE SERENE PASTORAL images, white picket fences, old log barns silver in the moonlight. An ornamental tin sun set high in the eaves of a farmhouse, tinstamped rays fanning upward. When the light subtly altered he saw that the pickets were stakes sharpened for impaling, something stirred in the strawstrewn hall of the barn, and there was a persistent ringing beyond the serrated treeline, the illogic of dreams imbued with dread. Then he became aware of Beth's leg flung across him in sleep, the smell of her hair, the ringing of the telephone, and he realized where he was, and that he wasn't a child after all.

He wondered how many times it had rung. Here in these clockless hours past midnight.

Hello.

It must have rung several for the voice was harsh and preemptory. I've got to have some help over here, she said.

What is it? He could hear the ragged hasp of her breathing.

I'm having some kind of attack. A heart attack.

All right. I'm on my way.

He was fumbling for his shoes. He found one sock, the other seemed to have vanished. Beth arose and he heard her stumbling toward the bathroom. Water running. He gave up on the sock and was hauling on his pants.

Your grandmother?

Yes.

Another heart attack?

He looked up. She was standing naked on the threshold of the bathroom, her face enigmatic in the dark bedroom, backlit by the bathroom light. Framed so against the yellow rectangle the light was a nimbus in her fair hair, and she seemed to be in flames.

Do you need me?

Stark and depthless against the light she looked like erotic statuary. Something in her hipslung posture lent her words an ambiguity he couldn't deal with just now, everything about her lately seemed subject to various interpretations.

I'll be back when I get back, he said. He slid his wallet and cigarettes into his pocket and went out.

He pushed the door back open. Lock the door, he told her, but she didn't say if she would or she wouldn't.

He drove out toward the farm, off the blacktop onto a cherted road so bowered by trees the moonlight couldn't defray the darkness, the road descended like a tunnel of black velvet, like a cleft in the earth itself he was driving off into. A whippoorwill swept up in the headlights, dark wings enormous, eyes wild and red as blood. Mailboxes, sleeping watch dogs, darkened houses shuttered against the night. Then the row of cedars, the lit farmhouse beyond them.

She was in the bentwood rocker. She sat twisted in agony. Her head in her hands, her breathing a thin panting.

Do you need an ambulance?

I've called it already. It should have been here.

Well, he said. He couldn't think of anything to say. It'd all been said before. Somewhere a clock ticked, a series of clocks deafening in the silence that stretched, stretched to a thin sharp wire. A tall grandfather clock whirred into life, gave three solemn and measured bongs.

I can't breathe. I've got to have some oxygen. Why won't they hurry up?

I think I hear them, he lied.

She was clutching her chest like a parody of agony. I'm on fire in here, she said. Behind the thick glasses her near colorless eyes were stricken, afraid. He felt a detached and impotent pity.

Is there anything I can do?

Get me a glass of orange juice. Maybe my sugar's gone down, I'm having some kind of attack.

He took a carton from the refrigerator and poured a glass of juice. He carried it to her. When she had drunk from the glass, he asked, Are you feeling any better?

Maybe a little.

Are you sure you want to go to the hospital? It never accomplished anything before. I can hire a nurse. I can stay myself.

I've already called it, she said. Something has got to be done. I'm not putting up with this.

He went out onto the porch. Where the porchlight tended away the yard lay silver in the moonlight, it glittered as if viewed through a veil of ice. Beyond it lay darkness, a veritable wall of insect sounds. From the ebony trees nightbirds called, cries so lost and forlorn he wondered what the configurations of such birds might be. Far up the road he could hear the whoop of the ambulance. Closer now homing down the walls of night. Its lights pulsed against the bowering trees like heat lightning. He lit a cigarette and waited.

The ambulance backed to the edge of the porch. An attendant leapt out and threw open the rear door and hauled out a gurney. Everything seemed rehearsed, every movement preordained, they'd been here before. Déjà vu all over again, he thought.

She needs oxygen, he said.

The driver came around and helped with the gurney. The paramedic took out a chromium oxygen bottle, a mask appended by a thin transparent tube. They seemed to have divined something unsaid from his face for their movements had become less hurried, more studied. He held the door open and they went into the living room with the gurney.

She seemed reassured by such an authoritative presence. The paramedic was kneeling at her feet adjusting gauges. The other had immediately commenced monitoring blood pressure, heartbeat. She was reaching for the mask. He could hear a thin hissing. Here you go,

Mrs. Wildman, the attendant said. You just relax now. She grasped the mask greedily the way a baby grasps its bottle, a drowning man a straw. As if the very essence of life itself had been distilled and concentrated in this chromium bottle, the ultimate spraycan.

They were already gently helping her onto the gurney, adjusting straps. Hand me my bag, she told Wildman. When he laid it beside her she clutched it possessively with a thin ravaged arm. They were rolling her through the doorway. I'll see you early in the morning, he said. The door creaked to on its keeperspring. Gurney wheels skirling across the oak porch. After a moment the rear door of the ambulance closed. The ambulance pulled away, siren shrieking, colored lights pulsing through the window, the wall across flickering in crimson neon. The wails grew faint and fainter and then he could hear whippoorwills calling one to the other.

Wildman sat in the room where he'd been a child. Where he'd crawled about the floors amongst his playthings. Images of himself at various ages adorned the walls, the table. He leant to study one. From across time the face seemed to be studying him back. Dark calm child with disaffected eyes. In the end time waylays you, he thought. It can outwait you, what does it care, it's got you outnumbered. There is just so damn much of it.

The room was begarbed with knickknacks, geegaws and ceramic cats and statuary he couldn't fathom the source of. They'd just accumulated with the years, so many years, had settled like dust motes out of time.

Across the room a bookcase where she kept the high school annuals. She'd been a teacher and she'd saved them all the way a traveler might save maps of places he'd been. Suddenly the room was claustrophobic, the walls were sliding inward on oiled tracks, he couldn't breathe. He put his cigarette out in a coffee cup and arose and went out into the night. Where the moon was a washedout ghost of itself and the sky was already faint with rosecolored light, the day lying somewhere east of him.

She's a hypochondriac, Beth said.

I guess, he said. He drank coffee.

What are you going to do about it?

Do about it?

You can't go on like this. All these emergencies in the middle of the night. You're not sleeping, it's too hard on you working construction the way you are this summer.

I'm used to it, he said. I can take it.

She ought to be thinking of you.

She's thinking about death, he said. It's staring her right in the face and she can't deal with it. I don't know if I could. Could you?

I can when I get that old, she said.

He watched her across the rim of his coffee cup. Dying seemed way down the line. She was fifteen years younger than he was. She was twenty five years old and her skin was poreless as marble and her mouth red and bruisedlooking. Her green eyes were the green of still deep waters and there was something arrogantly sexual about them, they said that she knew what she had and that she had an unlimited supply of it and it was going to last forever. He knew it wasn't and he wished he didn't.

She's old, he said. She can't teach anymore. She's sick and she's going to be sicker and then she's going to die. And she knows all that.

She'll outlive us all and dance on your grave, Beth said.

He set the cup down. Let's just give it a rest awhile, he said.

Are you going to work today?

It's Sunday.

I mean are you going to write.

I may. I don't know.

Why don't you write us another of those thousanddollar stories like you did that time, she said.

Thousanddollar stories don't grow on trees, he told her.

She smiled. It was gibberish to me anyway, she said.

I know. I saw your review in the paper.

Everybody's a critic, huh?

Everybody's a critic.

For a moment Beth and the old woman shared a curious duality, she had been a critic too.

I saw that piece in *The Atlantic*, his grandmother had said. I thought it offensive.

They liked it, he had told her. It was an Atlantic First Story.

It ought to have been an Atlantic last story. It was gibberish and obscene gibberish at that.

The world is obscene gibberish, Wildman said. I find it offensive.

She studied him. I liked you better as a child. You were such a lovable child.

The phone rang at four o'clock in the morning and there was a nurse on the line. Wildman lay listening to the nurse and to Beth's regular breathing beside him. She's had a rough night, the nurse said tentatively. She didn't sleep and she's had a lot of difficulty breathing. She insisted I call, she wants you to come.

He tried to think. He was still half asleep and tatters of his strange dreams swirled about him like eddies of brackish waters. I was just down there tonight, he said.

Well. I don't know anything about that. I just said I'd call.

He felt like a fool. A callous fool at that. I'm on my way, he said.

Highballing through the night at eighty five toward the little backwater town of Clifton where she carried all her medical business. Stringing past the barren ridges and the hollows where mist pooled white and opaque as snow. All these recent midnight runs had him feeling a denizen of the night himself, one of the whippoorwills of his childhood or the whores and drunks of his youth but he alone was still on the road. Civilization had pushed the whippoorwills deeper into the timber from where their cries came to him faint and ever fainter and the hands of the clock had pushed the whores and the drunks into each other's arms and into their dark and dreamless slumber. He strung past empty allnight markets alight with cool white fluorescence and past gas stations and abandoned lumber yards and the only soul he saw was the one glancing back from the rearview mirror.

The hospital itself seemed geared down for the night, humming along on half power. He hated hospitals and went stealthily down the gleaming tilefloored hall. Past doors opened and doors closed. Beyond these doors folks with their various ailments sleeping in their antiseptic cubicles if they could sleep and if not lying in a drug-induced stupor that passed for sleep in the regions. Like the larval stage of something dread waiting to be born and loosed upon an unsuspecting world.

She herself was still wide awake. They'd moved her to the pulmonary intensive care unit and she sat by the window waiting for day to come until she heard the door open then turning her head to see. Ravaged and wildlooking in her hospital gown she fixed him with eyes so fierce he had a thought for what halfcrazy stranger was inhabiting her body. A look of utter viciousness as if she held him and him alone responsible for the predicament in which she found herself. For the wearing out of irreplaceable organs, for the slow inevitable recession of the tide of blood, for life seeping away like night sewage, drop by septic drop.

Then the face changed and he laid an arm about her thin shoulders and she grasped his other arm with a hand more claws than fingers. She hung on fiercely, you'd not expect such a grip from one so frail. Instinctively he tried to pull away, the dying would take you with them if they could, it's dark down there and cold, a little company might lighten the tone of things.

Around midmorning he talked with her doctor. This doctor was young, Wildman considered him no more than a child. Styled blond hair, this wisp of a mustache. A preoccupied air. Wildman wondered was he competent. Perhaps he was a leech, a parasite, there was a pale vampirish look about him, a sucker of old folks' thin unhealthy blood.

She has anxiety attacks, the doctor said. I've tried to explain it to her. The emphysema makes it difficult for her to breathe and it scares her. The fear compounds the breathing problems and her heart trouble. Everything just compounds itself.

Is she going to die?

He shrugged. Well, she thinks she is. In the past weeks she's insisted on being tested for everything terminal. There's no reason she shouldn't live another five or ten years. She seems to be willing herself to die. How close are you to your grandmother?

Wildman shrugged. She raised me from a baby when my parents were killed in an accident. I guess that's pretty close.

Perhaps you could talk to her then. And there's no reason she has to be confined to a hospital. I'm releasing her later today.

I'll talk to her again, Wildman said. He smiled slightly. She taught school for fifty years. She's used to doing all the talking.

We're all going to die, the doctor said, as if this was some hot flash that hadn't caught up with Wildman yet and that he might want to make note of.

I'll tell her, he said politely. Sometimes there were windy gulfs of distance between what he thought and what he said and there was something mildly disturbing about it. He went out into the hall. It smelled of floor wax, antiseptic. He followed it to where he could see morning sunlight through a glass door and he went through the door into it. His senses were immediately assaulted by sensations: warmth, colors, the smell of the hot light falling through the green trees. Everything looked bright and gold and new and dying seemed very far away.

He hired a practical nurse and she stayed two nights which contained no phone calls and no midnight drives toward flashing ambulances then his grandmother fired her.

The nurse came and told him about it. He paid her off and drove out to the farm to see the old woman.

Why did you fire her, he wanted to know. You couldn't fire her anyway. I hired her.

She was a thief, the old woman said. She was stealing from me.

Stealing what?

My things, she said evasively. She waved an arm airily about the room. A motley of photographs, ceramic cats, plaster pickaninnies with fishing poles. I caught her stuffing them into her purse, she said.

Well, he said. He couldn't think of anything else to say.

I can stay by myself. I don't need her. I don't need you.

He lifted his shoulders in a shrug of defeat. You're three times seven. I guess you can do what you want to do.

I'm many more times seven than that, she said caustically. And I can't do anything I want to do. I can't even breathe God's own air like you and everyone else takes for granted. I'd give all that I own just to take a good deep breath.

She was kneeling astride him, moving above him in the halfdark. Head thrown back, yellow hair all undone. She was deeply tanned but her pale breasts bobbed like flowers. Her breath came ragged, like something feeding. Yet she was somehow unreal, like a fiercely evocative dream of lust.

The telephone rang.

Don't, she whispered urgently.

He reached for the phone and she grasped his arm and he jerked it away and the phone tipped off the nightstand. The ringing stopped and he could hear a tinny mechanical voice shrieking at him from the floor. Beth was laughing and wrestling him away from the phone and when he finally had the receiver against his ear he was still inside her and she began to move again.

Hello?

I've got to have some help over here.

He didn't say anything for a time. He listened to the disembodied wheeze of her breathing, the faint pumping of her ruined lungs.

All right, he said. I'm coming. He laid the phone down.

Beth was laughing helplessly. She collapsed against his chest, he could feel her taut nipples against his skin, they seemed to burn him. Her hair was all in her face, it smelled of flowers. Me too, she said and went into another burst of laughter. She was moving harder against him. He could feel himself inside her rigid and enormous, feel the slap of her flesh against his own. She had stopped laughing. I dare you to just take it out and go, she said. She rose above him light and graceful as smoke and he could feel her knees clamping his ribcage as if she were riding him, some succubus of the night riding him blind and fulltilt into the dark unknown, face in the wind and yellow hair strung out behind her. When she came she fell against him slack and boneless and he could feel her tiny teeth and her hot breath against his throat like a beast's.

The coffin was dark rosewood, an intricate pattern of flowers and vines carved or pressed into it and he couldn't help thinking it was what she would have grudgingly admitted was a fine piece of furniture. The woman within it on the satin pillow looked miraculously younger, no more than middleaged. As if death had peeled away the years like layers of dead skin. Her cares had fled and the skin relaxed and smoothed itself and her face had regained the primness of the longago schoolteacher. Most of all she just looked not there, absolutely gone, profoundly beyond any cruelty he might do her now or any kindness. From the hard oaken mourner's bench he watched this face and there were things he might have said to her had things been different but he willed himself to turn to stone inside.

When the preacher hushed they seemed to be at some pause in the procession of things: he didn't know what was expected of him but everything seemed preordained, dictated by ceremony. An attendant arose and closed the casket with an air of finality. He withdrew from his pocket a tool and began to tighten the screws that secured the lid. Wildman watched. It seemed to be an ordinary allen wrench. So arcane a use for so mundane a tool. Had its inventor had this purpose in mind? The pallbearers had arisen and taken their stations.

Following the casket down the aisle of the church Beth circled his waist with an arm as if she'd steady him in his grief and he was struck with a hot flash of annoyance. Did she think he'd fall prostrate and helpless, did she think he'd fly apart like a twodollar clock into a mass of springs and hands awry and useless unsequenced numbers?

They wound through the gravestones of older residents in this curious neighborhood of the dead toward the summit where raw earth waited. He felt tight and empty inside, his head airy and weightless, he felt as if he might go sailing up into the high thin cirrus. Folding chairs were set about and the green tent awning flapped in a sudden hot gust of summer wind.

He was working that summer with a construction crew laying bricks, work he'd done in his youth. Money seemed always short and the pay was good here and it supplemented his freelance income. He was five scaffolds up helping place walkboards and Rojo was taking a bucket of mortar off the winch. Rojo said, I've got to have some help over here.

This so startled Wildman that he stepped backward reflexively and there was nowhere to step save space. His heel caught a scaffold brace and tripped him and he was going headfirst and backward down the scaffolding. He grabbed at a brace whipping past but all it did was slow him, wrench his shoulder, half turn him in the air. He slammed into a sheet of plywood that capsized in a shower of dust and dried mortar and splintered brick. The plywood rebounded him onto the ground then slammed down onto him.

It had all happened in an instant but already he could hear voices, excited cries, running footsteps. He seemed to be slipping toward unconsciousness, black waters lapped at him. Man overboard, Wildman thought. Throw me one of them life preservers.

He opened his eyes. His vision was blurred. Somewhere some small critical adjustment was made, things came into focus. Colors weren't right though, everything seemed a dark muddy brown. The first thing he saw was a steeltoed workboot, the side serrated by a jagged sawcut.

He wiped blood off his forehead. Knifeblades of pain pierced his chest. There was a cut inside his mouth and he spat blood.

This flying shit is harder than it looks, he said.

Rojo drove him to the apartment building in a company pickup. Head bandaged, ribs tightly bound with some kind of swathing. He was beginning to hurt all over and the pills hadn't taken effect. He got out of the truck with some difficulty. He slammed the door and turned and Beth was standing on the wroughtiron stairway.

Good God, Buddy, she said. What happened to you?

He tried to fly off, Rojo told her. He was long on ambition but short on persistence. Just flopped his arms a time or two and give up and fell like a rock.

Good God, she said again. Her face in the white weight of the sun was flat and unreadable.

I'm all right, I'm all right, Wildman said.

You don't look so all right.

He's just bunged up some, Rojo said. They x-rayed everything he's got and none of it's busted. Ribs stove in a little. He'll be all right in a day or two. Ain't everybody can fall five scaffolds and not break nothing.

Beth had descended the stairway and she was helping Wildman onto the first steps. Hands of gentle solicitude.

You make it all right? Rojo called.

I'm all right, Wildman said. He wished he could think of something else to say. Everything he said sounded dull and halfwitted.

Halfway to the second floor there was a landing.

You want to sit down here and rest? I'll bring you a glass of iced tea.

He didn't want to say how all right he was. I'm just a little dizzy is all, he said.

Rest a minute.

Oh hell. Come on, I'm all right.

He drank the iced tea on the couch. She sat across from him in an armchair waiting as if an explanation or at least an elaboration of what had happened might be forthcoming but none was. He held the cold glass against his forehead. He closed his eyes. The room seemed to be tilting on an axis, everything poised at the point of sliding across the floor and slamming against the walls.

What made you fall?

He opened his eyes. The highvoltage pain pills seemed to be kicking in. She was moving away from him at the speed of light, the chair telescoping backward toward the receding wall. He tried to concentrate.

Gravity, he finally said.

When he awoke it was night. He wasn't on the couch anymore. He was in bed without knowing how he got there and she was reading on a chair by the wall sconce. He watched her. She read on, oblivious to his scrutiny. You won't keep her, a friend named Avery had told him. You can't keep her at home. She's used to being on the wing. One day she'll be a high fly in the tall weeds and that'll be all she wrote. Avery had wanted her himself, however, and this could hardly be considered an objective appraisal of the situation. Wildman had caught her on the rebound so quickly it made him dizzy, she had seemed to come with the thousanddollar story, the contract, the new agent, the dreams about the novel.

She had been with him three years but he had had to work full time at keeping her. He began to think of her as some piece of expensive and highpowered machinery he had bought on time. Some luxurious automobile loaded with options and coated with twenty coats of lacquer but the payments were eating him alive, the payments were enormous with a balloon at the end and he had begun to think he couldn't keep them current. He hadn't been trying as hard lately, he'd been slacking off, and the threat of repossession hung over his head like a guillotine on a frayed rope. Long a student of nuance he had noticed a difference in her body language when other men glanced at her, a speculative look of distance in her eyes when she studied him. He caught her appraising herself critically in a mirror as if she were evaluating herself, looking for microscopic signs of wear and tear.

After a while she seemed to feel the cool weight of his eyes and she looked up. She closed the book and laid it aside.

How do you feel?

Like death warmed over, he said. My ribs hurt. I can't take a deep breath. I can't even breathe God's own air like everybody else.

What?

Nothing.

You're acting awfully strange lately.

Strange in what way?

Strange in a lot of ways. Half the time you act as if you're not even here. You don't talk to me. You talk but it's like little things you say for your own amusement. You're off in a little world of your own. You used to act like this sometimes when you were writing but you're not writing. I don't understand you anymore.

I don't know, he said.

You don't know what?

I don't know what you're talking about. I apologize for all my shortcomings. My ribs do hurt though.

You want to go out and eat? It's early yet.

No. I don't feel like it and anyway I'm not hungry.

Go back to sleep then, she said. She took up the book and opened it. She sat as if she was reading but he didn't think she was. He closed his eyes.

After a while he opened them and she was watching him. This shit is beginning to get on my nerves, she said.

I don't know that I'm crazy about it myself, Wildman said.

The next morning he sat on the sunlit balcony wearing dark glasses and watching the comings and goings of the apartment building. Across the parking lot a yellow moving van was backed up to an apartment and two men were wrestling an enormous green sofa into its belly. Folks brought out boxes, cartons, a woman carried a lamp.

So many comings and goings, folks moving in, folks moving out. There seemed little permanence left to the world. Families split and regrouped. People threw up their hands and carried their lives back to ground zero and began again. People were perpetually changing jobs, changing partners, changing lives.

His head throbbed dully. He chewed two Excedrin and swallowed them, hot sour aftertaste in the back of his mouth. The rental van pulled onto the highway, headed toward the interstate. Log trucks passed in a blue haze of diesel smoke, concrete trucks, mixer spinning slowly. They were cutting all the timber, paving the world with concrete.

Beth, he called.

She came to the door and halfopened it, he could see her, warpedlooking through the glass.

What is it?

You want to drive out to the farm?

The farm? What on earth for?

Just to look around a little. Anyway it's mine now. Ours.

Ours? You can have my part of it. That place gives me the shivers. Like something walking over my grave.

All it needs is a little work.

All it needs is a hole dug beside it and a bulldozer to push it off in the hole and somebody to throw in the dirt. That's what it needs.

Well. Such as it is it's mine. I thought I might clean up a little. Pack up some of her things. I don't know what I'm going to do with all that stuff.

Dig a bigger hole, Beth said.

I need to pick up some magazines anyhow. Is there anything I can get for you?

Nothing you can find in a 7-11, she said. She paused. He was halfway down the wrought iron stairway when she said, You're even beginning to look like her.

He didn't turn.

Buddy, she called.

He halted. What?

She was silent a time. Nothing, she finally said. He went on.

He sat in a welter of cardboard cartons and strewn memorabilia. It was hopeless. There was just so much of it. The room seemed time's attic, its dump heap. Finally he gave up. The old woman saturated the very walls, her spirit was not going to be exorcised by a few cardboard boxes, she was not going to be dispossessed.

She had seemed intent on absorbing him, secreting some sort of subtle chemical that was digesting him, making him part of her. Eating him alive. Every move he made came under her critical scrutiny.

That Luna girl is no good for you, she had told him once in his junior year.

Well. I think she is. That's for me to decide.

I knew her whole family. There wasn't anything to any of them. None of them ever amounted to a hill of beans. She's in some of my classes. She lets the boys look up her dress.

He hadn't known what to say to that and so had said nothing at all. He figured it'd all blow over. But she had gone over there. She had a talk with Mrs. Luna and the next time he had gone calling he was left cooling his heels on the porch fifteen minutes before Mrs. Luna even opened the door and he was turned away with polite and distant firmness.

Lynell had never spoken to him again but he had seen her whispering once to another girl and both of them were looking at him and he wondered what was being said. He never found out what his grandmother and Mrs. Luna had discussed and on some level he didn't want to know.

And yet.

She'd nursed him through all the childhood diseases, mumps and whooping cough and measles, stood between him and fire and plague and biting dogs. She sheltered him from the world.

Which at the first opportunity he'd escaped into with a vengeance, feeling that if she was so down on it it couldn't be all bad.

He sat on the sunward side of the porch in an old lounge chair, eyes closed behind the dark glasses. He didn't have to see anyway, it was all burnt into memory. Eastward lay thick timber she'd never allowed cut, a deep primeval tangle of cypress and liveoak, from this distance lush and romantic as a nineteenth century painting. He'd wandered there as a child, alone but not lonely, spent whole days dreaming there, watched her from the rim of the wood as she walked across the stubbled field, her clothing pale and spectral in the waning day. You Buddy, she'd call. You get yourself over here. It's suppertime.

When he returned to the apartment complex dusk had already begun to deepen and the western sky beyond the angular brick skyline was mottled red as blood. The first thing he noticed was that the canary yellow Mustang he'd bought Beth was gone. He gathered up the magazines and went up the stairs. Somehow he knew what he was going to find.

She was gone. Not only Beth but every vestige of Beth, her clothes and personal possessions, even the book she'd been reading. She was gone as completely as if she had never been, and for a dizzy moment he wondered if she had. If he'd ever smelled her hair, kissed her bruisedlooking mouth. She was gone like a high fly in the tall weeds, like a bird on the wing, and search as he might there was nothing to prove she had ever been, not so much as a lipsticked cigarette butt, or a snarl of blonde hair curled like a sleeping newt in the bathroom drain.

In his dream he was a child being led down a winding country road. It was early morning and he could feel the dew on his bare feet and the grasses and weeds were damp. They went by grazing cows and deep woods that still held night at their center, he could see slashes of it through the trees. The hand clasping his own child's hand was gentle, the way was long but he did not tire. A hawk flew from the roadside with a flurry of wings and he glanced to the side and saw that there was no one beside him. A hand bewenned and agespotted still clutched his own and he could feel the delicate tubelike bones beneath the slack skin, feel a wedding band on the ring finger and glancing up he saw that the disembodied arm tended upward, and upward, a thin wasted arm in lavender brocade that stretched to infinity, to high thin clouds that ultimately obscured it.

The ringing phone woke him. Beth? he thought, but the voice in his ear was harsh and preemptory, curiously mechanical, like something electronic imitating a voice. It said, I've got to have some help over here.

He felt numb, cold as ice. Who is this? he asked. Is this your idea of a joke? Yet in some curious cobwebbed corner of his mind there was a part of him that was waiting for just such a phone call, had been for days. He exhaled, he'd breathed deeper than he meant to, the sudden pain made him gasp. But some release had been negotiated, some delicate border had been broached, he was already feeling about for his shoes.

He drove through the cool summer night, everyone asleep, the highway his alone. At home with the night now, at peace. When he left the blacktop the lowering trees beckoned him into the tunnel of darkness like a vaguely erotic promise. And it was like a road that wound down through time.

Beyond the blurred cedars the farmhouse sat foursquare in the moonlight, its tin roof gleaming wetly with dew, its windows enigmatic and dark. Steeply gabled, its high eaves rose in black and silver shadows, its ornate oldfashioned tin cornicing somehow stately and dignified. A bisected tin sun was set high in the eaves, tin rays fanning upward, you hardly ever saw Victorian trim like this anymore.

He went up the brick walk to the wraparound porch, the silence was enormous, the house seemed to be listening to some sound that hadn't reached him yet. He felt for his keys. When the door was unlocked it opened silently inward on oiled hinges and he stepped into the darkness. Hot stifling darkness with compounded smells, jasmine, Vick's Vaporub, time itself. From the kitchen the refrigerator hummed, somewhere a clock ticked with a firm strong heartbeat. He turned on the light and the first thing he looked for was the telephone. It was cradled and when he took it up all there was to hear was a dialtone.

He sat in the bentwood rocker. He lit a cigarette. She had been lying on her left side before the rocker, about where his feet were now. Beside the rocker was a table where he'd restacked the copies of National Geographic, the goldrimmed bifocals. Even after all that time she had still been breathing shallowly and he had squatted there with the phone in his hand watching her. Her breath was a thin panting, like a dying kitten he remembered from childhood. Finally she had exhaled and just never took another breath.

The ramifications of what he'd done or not done were dizzying, he'd made a lifetime out of living on the edge but this time he'd slipped and fallen further than he'd ever meant to go. It ain't everybody can fall five scaffolds and not break nothing, Rojo had said. What had she thought when everything began to shut down? Whole banks of memory rendered into oblivion, had she seen the little night watchman going from room to room throwing breakers, clicking his flashlight down the dark corridors, will the last one out turn out the light?

She seemed to hover the room yet, dusting the bric-a-brac, straightening the giltframed photograph of some ancestor whose bones had gone to dust. Most of the photographs were of Wildman though and they charted his growth from infancy to adulthood like graphs showing the evolution of a species. One of a toddler sitting in a childsize rocker, a disembodied grandmother's hand on his shoulder and all there was of the young Wildman left was the dark and haunted eyes that studied this likeness.

He went into the kitchen and turned on the light. He made a cup of instant Nescafe from the hot water tap and went with the cup in his hand through the kitchen door into what had been the living room and he saw with a stricken wonder that everything had changed forever.

The rosewood coffin on its catafalque set against the west wall where the sofa had always been. The casket and its occupant seemed to dwarf the room and were twinned by the opaque window behind it. He approached it, stared down at the stern old woman with irongrey hair and pincenez. Every detail was stored in his mind with a clinical detachment. The prim pursed mouth was slacker now, a stitch had given and left a small bloodless incision, he could see the wadded cotton or whatever her mouth was packed with. Studying her so intently he saw with a dull loathing a faint blue pulse beating in her throat.

He stumbled numbly backward over a folding chair. He saw with no surprise that the room had been set about with such chairs all alike stamped McFarland Funeral Home. He righted the one he'd stumbled over and seated himself like a patient spectator awaiting the commencement of some arcane show.

He sat waiting for time to draw on. In truth time had ceased to exist, neither past nor future, all motion had slowed finally to a drugged halt and all there was at the end of the world was an old woman in a casket and a man watching with heavylidded eyes from a folding chair. Then there was a faint rustle of funeral silk, the smell of lemon verbena, and the old woman raised her head. Cocked slightly sidewise in an attitude of listening. Then a scarcely audible sigh, and she pillowed her head again on the quilted satin. The clock in the corner began to toll, one, two, three, twelve times in all and she raised herself again, pulling herself upright with a clawed hand on the edge of the casket, tendons pulled taut as wires with exertion. She turned toward the window, listening intently. He knew intuitively that she was listening for him, or for what he had once been, an eighteen year old Wildman that always had to be home by midnight.

He heard the sound of an automobile approaching, headlights slid whitely across the wall, ceased and vanished. The engine died. The old woman sank back to rest with an expression of satisfaction. The clock began to strike again, tolled on and on, turning to see he watched its hands ratcheting madly backward, he could hear the protesting grind of metal on metal, gears and pins and springs being sheared off and broken. When the hands ceased at six o'clock the old woman began to rise again and the room was saturated with the smell of brewing coffee, he could hear it singing in the glasstopped percolator, he could smell bacon sizzling in hot grease. In the kitchen pots and pans rattled, cutlery was being laid out. Outside a car door slammed, a dog dead these twenty years scrabbled up from the porch and went running to meet its master. The smells of coffee and bacon intensified, became overpowering, a corrupt stench of charred meat.

The air was tinged with greasy smoke, somewhere flames were crackling like something feeding. He turned toward the kitchen. Beyond the door was a strobic flickering like summer lightning and thick black smoke rolled along the floor. There was a step on the porch. Someone was approaching the door, he could hear the dog leaping and whining to be petted. Flames were darting up and down the wallpaper playfully and the rug beneath his feet buckled and began to smoke, ceramic cats warped and ran like melting glass, the very air was aflame.

He took a deep breath and sucked in pure fire. The flesh of his lungs seared and crackled and burst with thin hisses of steam. The last sound he heard was the screendoor opening on its keeperspring and then everything fell from him in a rush, Beth and the thousanddollar story and the midnight runs to Clifton and every detail of his life that had made him Buddy Wildman and no other. Years reeled backward in a dizzying rush and abruptly he was on the floor, a naked child crawling about the bubbling linoleum, hair ablaze and swaddled in fire, feeling about for his playthings amongst the painted flames.

Time Done Been Won't Be No More

WHERE WILL YOU GO WHEN YOUR SKIN CANNOT CONTAIN YOU?

THE JEEPSTER COULDN'T KEEP STILL. For forty-eight hours he's been steady on the move and no place worked for long. He'd think of somewhere to be and go there and almost immediately suck the life from it, he could feel it charring around him. He felt he was on fire and running with upraised arms into a stiff cold wind but instead of cooling him the wind just fanned the flames. His last so-called friend had faded on him and demanded to be left by the roadside with his thumb in the air.

The Jeepster drove westward into a sun that had gone down the sky so fast it left a fiery wake like a comet. Light pooled above the horizon like blood and red light hammered off the hood of the SUV he was driving. He put on his sunglasses. In the failing day the light was falling almost horizontally and the highway glittered like some virtual highway in a fairy tale or nightmare.

His so-called friend had faded because The Jeepster was armed and dangerous. He was armed and dangerous and running on adrenaline and fury and grief and honed to such a fine edge that alcohol and drugs no longer affected him. Nothing worked on him. He had a pocket full of money and nine-millimeter automatic shoved into the waistband of his jeans and his T-shirt pulled down over it. He had his ticket punched for the graveyard or the penitentiary and one foot on the platform and the other foot on the train. He had everything he needed to get himself killed, to push the borders back and alter the very geography of reality itself.

On the outskirts of Ackerman's Field the neon of a Texaco station bled into the dusk like a virulent stain. Night was falling like some disease he was in the act of catching. At the pumps he filled the SUV up and watched the traffic accomplish itself in a kind of wonder. Everyone should have been frozen in whatever attitude they'd held when the hammer fell on Aimee and they should hold that attitude forever. He felt like a plague set upon the world to cauterize and cleanse it.

He went through the pneumatic door. He had his Ray-Bans shoved on the top of his shaven head and he was grinning his gap-toothed grin. Such patrons as were about regarded him warily. He looked like bad news. He looked like the letter edged in black, the telegram shoved under your door at three o'clock in the morning.

You seen that Coors man? The Jeepster asked the man at the register.

Seen what? The man asked. Somewhere behind them a cue stick tipped a ball and it went down the felt in a near-silent hush and a ball rattled into a pocket and spiraled down and then there was just silence.

The Jeepster laid money on the counter. I know all about that Coors man, he said. I know Escue was broke and he borrowed ten bucks off the Coors man for the gas to get to where Aimee was working. Where's he at?

The counterman made careful change. He don't run today, he said. Wednesday was the last day he's been here. And what if he did run, what if he was here? How could he know? He was just a guy doing Escue a favor. He didn't know.

He didn't know, he didn't know. The Jeepster said. You reckon that'll keep the dirt out of his face? I don't.

They regarded each other in silence. The Jeepster picked up his change and slid it into his pocket. He leaned toward the counterman until their faces were very close together. Could be you chipped in a few bucks yourself, he finally said.

Just so you know, the counterman said, I've got me a sawed-off here under the counter. And I got my hand right on the stock. You don't look just right to me. You look crazy. You look like you escaped from prison or the crazy house.

I didn't escape, The Jeepster said. They let me out and was glad to see me go. They said I was too far gone, they couldn't do anything for me. They said I was a bad influence.

The Jeepster in Emile's living room. Emile was thinking this must be the end-time, the end of days. The rapture with graves bursting open and folk sailing skyward like superheroes. There was no precedent for this. The

Jeepster was crying. His shaven head was bowed. His fingers were knotted at the base of his skull. A letter on each finger, LOVE and HATE inscribed there by some drunk or stoned tattooist in blurred jailhouse blue. The fingers were interlocked illegibly and so spelled nothing. The Jeepster's shoulders jerked with his sobbing, there was more news to read on his left arm: HEAVEN WON'T HAVE ME AND HELL'S AFRAID I'M TAKING OVER.

Emile himself had fallen on hard times. Once the scion of a prosperous farm family, now he could only look back on long-lost days that were bathed in an amber haze of nostalgia. He'd inherited all this and for a while there were wonders. Enormous John Deere cultivators and hay balers and tractors more dear than Rolls-Royces. For a while there was coke and crank and wild parties. Friends unnumbered and naked women rampant in their willingness to be sent so high you couldn't have tracked them on radar, sports cars that did not hold up so well against trees and bridge abutments.

Little by little Emile had sold things off for pennies on the dollar and day by day the money rolled through his veins and into his lungs and the greasy coins trickled down his throat. The cattle were sold away or wandered off. Hogs starved and the strong ate the weak. It amazed him how easily a small fortune could be pissed away. Money don't go nowhere these days, Emile said when he was down to selling off stepladders and drop cords.

Finally he was down to rolling his own, becoming an entrepreneur, slaving over his meth lab like some crazed alchemist at his test tubes and brazier on the brink of some breakthrough that would cleanse the world of sanity forever.

The appalled ghost of Emile's mother haunted these rooms, hovered fretfully in the darker corners. Wringing her spectral hands over doilies beset with beer cans and spilled ashtrays. Rats tunneling in secret trespass through the upholstery. There were man-shaped indentations in the sheetrocked walls, palimpsest cavities with outflung arms where miscreants had gone in drunken rage. JESUS IS THE UNSEEN LISTENER TO EVERY CONVERSATION, an embroidered sampler warned from the wall. There were those of Emile's customers who wanted it taken down or turned to the wall. Emile left it as it was. He needs an education, Emile would say. He needs to know what it's like out here in the world. There's no secrets here.

The Jeepster looked up. He took off his Ray-Bans and shook his head as if to clear it of whatever visions beset it. Reorder everything as you might shake a kaleidoscope into a different pattern.

You got to have something, he said.

I ain't got jack shit.

Pills or something. Dilaudid.

I ain't got jack shit. I'm out on bond, and I done told you they're watchin this place. A sheriff's car parks right up there in them trees. Takin pictures. I seen some son of a bitch with a video camera. It's like being a fuckin movie star. Man can't step outside to take a leak without windin up on videotape or asked for an autograph.

What happened?

I sent Qualls to Columbia after a bunch of medicine for my lab. He kept tryin to buy it all at the same drugstore. Like I specifically told him not to do. He'd get turned down and go on to the next drugstore. Druggists kept callin the law and callin the law. By the time they pulled him over it looked like a fuckin parade. Cops was fightin over who had priorities. He had the whole backseat and trunk full of Sudafed and shit. He rolled over on me and here they come with a search warrant. I'm out on bond.

I can't stand this.

I guess you'll have to, Emile said. Look, for what it's worth I'm sorry for you. And damn sorry for her. But I can't help you. Nobody can. You want to run time back and change the way things happened. But time won't run but one way.

I can't stand it. I keep seeing her face.

Well.

Maybe I'll go back out there to the funeral home and see her.

Maybe you ought to keep your crazy ass away from her daddy. You'll remember he's a cop.

I have to keep moving. I never felt like this. I never knew you could feel like this. I can't be still. It's like I can't stand it in my own skin.

Emile didn't say anything. He looked away. To the window where the night-mirrored glass turned back their images like sepia desperadoes in some old daguerreotype.

You still got that tow bar or did you sell it?

What?

I'm fixing to get that car. Aimee's car. Pull it off down by the river somewhere.

This is not makin a whole lot of sense to me.

They wouldn't let me in out there, they won't even let me in to see her body. I went and looked at her car. Her blood's all in the seat. On the windshield. It's all there is of her left in the world I can see or touch. I aim to have it.

Get away from me, Emile said.

Aimee had turned up at his place at eight o'clock in the morning. The Jeepster still slept, it took the horn's insistent blowing to bring him in the jeans he'd slept in out onto the porch and into a day where a soft summer rain fell.

Her battered green Plymouth idled in the yard. He stood on the porch a moment studying it. In the night a spider had strung a triangular web from the porch beam and in its ornate center a single drop of water clung gleaming like a stone a jeweler had set. The Jeepster went barefoot down the doorsteps into the muddy yard.

He was studying the car. Trying to get a count on the passengers. He couldn't tell until she cranked down the glass that it was just Aimee. He stood with his hands in his pockets listening to the rhythmic swish of the windshield wipers. The dragging stutter of a faulty wiper blade.

I need a favor, she said.

It had been awhile and he just watched her face. She had always had a sly, secretive look that said, I'll bet you wish you had what I have, know what I know, could share the dreams that come for me alone when the day winds down and the light dims and it is finally quiet. She was still darkly pretty but there was something different about her. The grain of her skin, but especially the eyes. Something desperate hiding there in the dark shadows and trying to peer out. She already looked like somebody sliding off the face of the world.

I don't have a thing. I'm trying to get off that shit.

Really?

I've had the dry heaves and the shakes. Fever. Cramps and the shits. Is that real enough for you? Oh yeah, and hallucinations. I've had them. I may be having one now. I may be back in the house with baby monkeys running up and down the window curtains.

She made a dismissive gesture, a slight curling of her upper lip. Will you do me a favor or not?

Is Escue all out of favors?

I've left him, I'm not going back. He's crazy.

No shit. Did a light just go on somewhere?

He stays on that pipe and it's fucked him up or something. His head. You can't talk to him.

I wouldn't even attempt it.

I don't understand goddamn men. Live with them and they think they own you. Want to marry you. Eat you alive. Jimmy was older and he'd been around and I thought he wouldn't be so obsessive. Sleep with him a few times and it's the same thing over again. Men.

The Jeepster looked away. Blackbirds rose from the field in a fury of wings and their pattern shifted and shifted again as if they sought some design they couldn't quite attain. He thought about Aimee and men. He knew she'd slept with at least one man for money. He knew it for a fact. The Jeepster himself had brokered the deal.

What you get for taking up with a son of a bitch old enough to be your daddy.

I see you're still the same. The hot shit macho man. The man with the platinum balls. You'd die before you'd ask me to come back, wouldn't you?

You made your bed. Might as well spoon up and get comfortable.

Then I want to borrow a gun.

What for?

I'm afraid he'll be there tonight when I get off work. He said he was going to kill me and he will. He slapped me around some this morning. I just want him to see it. If he knows I've got it there in my purse he'll leave me alone.

I'm not loaning you a gun.

Leonard.

You'd shoot yourself. Or some old lady crossing the street. Is he following you?

He's broke. I don't think he's got the gas.

I hope he does turn up here and tries to slap me around some. I'll drop him where he stands and drag his sorry, woman-beating ass inside the house and call the law.

Loan me the pistol. You don't know how scared I am of him. You don't know what it's like.

The loop tape of some old blues song played in his head: *You don't know my, you don't know my, you don't know my mind.*

No. I'll pick you up from work. I'll be there early and check out the parking lot and if he's there I'll come in and tell you. You can call the cops. You still working at that Quik Mart?

Yes. But you won't come.

I'll be there.

Can I stay here tonight?

You come back you'll have to stay away from Escue. I won't have him on the place. Somebody will die.

I'm done with him.

The Jeepster looked across the field. Water was standing in the low places and the broken sky lay there reflected. Rain crows called from tree to tree. A woven-wire fence drowning in honeysuckle went tripping toward the horizon, where it vanished in mist like the palest of smoke.

Then you can stay all the nights there are, he said.

The murmur of conversation died. Folks in the General Café looked up when The Jeepster slid into a booth but when he stared defiantly around they went back to studying their plates and shoveling up their food. There was only the click of forks and knives, the quickstep rubber-soled waitresses sliding china across formica.

He ordered chicken-fried steak and chunky mashed potatoes and string beans and jalapeno cornbread. He sliced himself a bite of steak and began to chew. Then he didn't know what to do with it. Panic seized him. The meat grew in his mouth, a gristly, glutinous mass that forced his jaws apart, distorted his face. He'd forgotten how to eat. He sat in wonder. The bite was supposed to go somewhere but he didn't know where. What came next, forgetting to breathe? Breathing out when he should be breathing in, expelling the oxygen and hanging on to the carbon dioxide until the little lights flickered dim and dimmer and died.

He leaned and spat the mess onto his plate and rose. Beneath his T-shirt the outlined gun was plainly visible. He looked about the room. Their switchblade eyes flickered away. He stood for an awkward moment surveying them as if he might address the room. Then he put too much money on the table and crossed the enormity of the tile floor and went out the door into the trembling dusk.

So here he was again, The Jeepster back at the same old stand. On his first attempt he'd almost made it to the chapel where she lay in state before a restraining hand fell on his shoulder, but this time they were prepared. Two uniformed deputies unfolded themselves from their chairs and approached him one on either side. They turned him gently, one with an arm about his shoulders.

Leonard, he said. It's time to go outside. Go on home now. You can't come in here.

The deputy was keeping his voice down but the father had been waiting for just this visitor. The father in his khakis rose up like some sentry posted to keep the living from crossing the border into the paler world beyond. A chair fell behind him. He had to be restrained by his brothers in arms, the sorriest and saddest of spectacles. He voice was a rusty croak. Crying accusations of ruin and defilement and loss. All true. He called curses down upon The Jeepster, proclaiming his utter worthlessness, asking, no, demanding, that God's lightning burn him incandescent in his very footsteps.

As if superstitious, or at any rate cautious, the cops released him and stepped one step away. One of them opened the door and held it. Doors were always opening, doors were always closing. The Jeepster went numbly through this opening into the hot volatile night and this door fell to behind him like a thunderclap.

In these latter days The Jeepster had discovered an affinity for the night side of human nature. Places where horrific events had happened drew him with a gently perverse gravity. These desecrated places of murder and suicide had the almost-nostalgic tug of his childhood home. The faces of the perpetrators looked vaguely familiar, like long-lost kin he could but barely remember.

These were places where the things that had happened were so terrible that they had imprinted themselves onto an atmosphere that still trembled faintly with the unspeakable.

The rutted road wound down and down. Other roads branched off this one and others yet, like capillaries bleeding off civilization into the wilderness, and finally he was deep in the harrikin.

Enormous trees rampant with summer greenery reared out of the night and loomed upon the windshield and slipstreamed away. All day the air had been hot and humid and to the west a storm was forming. Soundless lightning flickered the horizon to a fierce rose, then trembled and vanished. The headlights froze a deer at the height of its arc over a strand of barbed wire like a holographic deer imaged out of The Jeepster's mind or the free-floating ectoplasm of the night.

He parked before the dark bulk of a ruined farmhouse. Such windows as remained refracted the staccato lightning. Attendant outbuildings stood like hesitant, tree-shadowed familiars.

He got out. There was the sound of water running somewhere. Off in the darkness fireflies arced like sparks thrown off by the heat. He had a liter of vodka in one hand and a quart of orange juice in the other. He drank and then sat for a time on a crumbling stone wall and studied the house. He had a momentary thought for copperheads in the rocks but he figured whatever ran in his veins was deadlier than any venom and any snake that bit him would do so at its peril. He listened to the brook muttering to itself. Night birds called from the bowered darkness of summer trees. He drank again and past the gleaming ellipse of the upraised bottle the sky bloomed with the bloodred fire and after a moment thunder rumbled like voices in a dream and a wind was at the trees.

He set aside the orange juice and went back to the SUV and took a flashlight from the glove box. Its beam showed him a fallen barn, wind-writhed trees, the stone springhouse. Beneath the springhouse a stream trilled away over tumbled rocks and vanished at the edge of the flashlight's beam. You had to stoop to enter the stone door, it was a door for gnomes or little folk. The interior had the profound stillness of a cathedral, the waiting silence of a church where you'd go to pray.

This was where they'd found the farmer after he'd turned the gun on himself. Why here? What had he thought about while he'd waited for the courage to eat the barrel of the shotgun? The Jeepster turned involuntarily and spat. There was a cold metallic taste of oil in his mouth.

Light slid around the walls. Leached plaster, water beading and dripping on the concrete, the air damp and fetid. A black-spotted salamander crouched on its delicate toy feet and watched him with eyes like bits of obsidian. Its leathery orange skin looked alien to this world.

Against the far wall stood a crypt shaped stone spring box adorned with curling moss like coarse, virid maidenhair. He trailed a hand in the icy water. In years long past, here was where they'd kept their jugged milk. Their butter. He'd have bet there was milk and butter cooling here the day it all went down. When the farmer walked in on his wife and brother in bed together. The Jeepster could see it. Overalls hung carefully on a bedpost. Worn gingham dress folded just so. Did he kill them then or watch awhile? But The Jeepster knew, he was in the zone. He killed them then. And lastly himself, a story in itself.

When The Jeepster came back out, the storm was closer and the thunder constant and the leaves of the clashing trees ran like quicksilver. He drank from the vodka and climbed high steep steps to the farmhouse porch and crossed it and hesitated before the open front door. The wind stirred drifted leaves of winters past. The oblong darkness of the doorway seemed less an absence of light than a tangible object, a smooth glass rectangle so solid you could lay a hand on it. Yet he passed through it into the house. There was a floral scent of ancient funerals. The moving light showed him dangling sheaves of paper collapsed from the ceiling, wallpaper of dead faded roses. A curled and petrified work shoe like a piece of proletarian sculpture.

The revenants had eased up now to show The Jeepster about. A spectral hand to the elbow, solicitously guiding him to the bedroom. Hinges grated metal on metal. A hand, pointing. There. Do you see? He nodded. The ruined bed, the hasty, tangled covers, the shot-riddled headboard. Turning him, the hand again pointing. There. Do you see? Yes, he said. The empty window opening on nothing save darkness. The Jeepster imagined the mad scramble over the sill and out the window, the naked man fleeing toward the hollow, pistoned legs pumping, buckshot shrieking after him like angry bees, feets don't fail me now.

The Jeepster clicked out the light. He thought of the bloodstained upholstery strewn with pebbled glass and it did not seem enough. Nothing seemed enough. He stood for a time in the darkness, gathering strength from these lost souls for what he had to do.

He lay in the backseat of the SUV and tried to sleep. Rain pounded on the roof, wind-shipped rain rendered the glass opaque and everything beyond these windows a matter of conjecture. The vodka slept on his chest like a stuffed bear from childhood. It hadn't worked anyway, it might as well have been tap water. Things would not leave him alone, old unheeded voices plagued his ears. Brightly colored images tumbled through his mind. An enormous, stained-glass serpent had shattered inside him and was moving around blindly reassembling itself.

He'd concentrate on more pleasant times, his senior year in high school. He saw his leaping body turning in the air, the football impossibly caught as if by legerdemain, he heard the crowd calling his name. But a scant few years later he was seated alone in the empty stands with a bottle between his feet. A winter wind blew scraps of paper and turned paper cups against the frozen ground and the lush green playing field had turned brittle and bare. He wondered if there was a connection between these two images and, further, what that connection might be.

A picture of himself and Aimee the first time, try to hold onto this one, fooling around on her bed. Her giggling against his chest. A new urgency in her lips and tongue. Leonard, quit. Quit. Oh quit. Oh. Then he was inside her and her gasp was muffled by applause from the living room and her father chuckling at the Letterman show. Other nights, other beds. The Jeepster and Aimee shared a joint history, tangled and inseparable, like two trees that have grown together, a single trunk faulted at the heart.

Drink this, smoke this, takes these. Hell, take his money, you won't even remember it in the morning. You'll never see him again. Ruin, defilement, loss. One pill makes you larger, one pill makes you small, one pill puts you on the road to Clifton with a Ford truck riding your bumper.

For here's what happened, or what happened on the surface, here's what imprinted itself on the very ether and went everywhere at once, the news the summer wind whispered in The Jeepster's sleeping ear.

The truck pulled up on Aimee past Centre, Escue blew the truck horn, pounded on the steering wheel. She rolled down the glass and gave him the finger. She sped up. He sped up. She could see his twisted face in the rearview mirror. The round O of his mouth seemed to be screaming soundlessly.

When she parked on the lot before the Quik Mart he pulled in beside her. He was out of the Ford before it quit rocking on its springs. He had a 457 magnum in his hand. As he ran around the hood of his truck she was trying to get out of her car on the passenger's side. Just as he shot out the driver's side window the passenger door on the Plymouth flew open and she half fell onto the pavement. She was on her back with her right elbow on the pavement and a hand to her forehead.

She looked as if she might be raking the hair out of her eyes. He shot her twice in the face. Somebody somewhere began to scream.

Hey. Hey goddamn it.

A man came running out of the Quik Mart with a pistol of his own. His feet went slap slap slap on the pavement. Escue turned and leveled the pistol and fired. The running man dropped to his palms and behind him the plate glass window of the Quik Mart dissolved in a shimmering waterfall.

The man was on his hands and knees feeling about for his dropped weapon when Escue put the barrel of the revolver in his own mouth with the sight hard against his palate and pulled the trigger.

Now The Jeepster opened the door of the SUV and climbed out into the rain. He raised his arms to the windy heavens. All about him turmoil and disorder. Rain came in torrents and the thunder cracked like gunfire and lightning walked among the vibratory trees. His shaven head gleamed like a rain-washed stone. He seemed to be conducting the storm with his upraised arms. He demanded the lightning take him but it would not.

Mouse-quiet and solemn. The Jeepster crossed the rich mauve carpet. Who knows what hour, the clock didn't exist that could measure times like these. This time there were no laws stationed to intercept him and he passed unimpeded into another chamber. Soft, indirect lighting fell on purple velvet curtains tied back with golden rope. He moved like an agent provocateur through the profoundest of silences.

The chamber was furnished with a steel gray casket, wherein an old man with a caved face and a great blade of a nose lay in state. Two middle-aged female mourners sat in folding chairs and watched The Jeepster's passage with fearful, tremulous eyes.

He parted another set of purple curtains. Here the room was empty save for a pale pink casket resting on a catafalque. He crossed the room and stood before it. Water dripped from his clothing onto the carpet. A fan whirred somewhere.

After a while he knew someone was standing behind him. He'd heard no footsteps but he turned to face an old man in worn, dusty black hunched in the back like a vulture, maroon tie at his throat. His thin hair was worn long on the side and combed over his bald pate. The Jeepster could smell his brilliantined hair, the talcum that paled his cheeks.

The Jeepster could tell the old man wanted to order him to leave but was afraid to. The old man didn't want to be here. He wanted to be ten thousand miles away, in some world so far away even the constellations were unknowable and the language some unintelligible gobbledygook no human ear could decipher. He wished he'd retired yesterday.

For The Jeepster looked bad. He was waterlogged and crazed and the pistol was outside his shirt now and his eyes were just the smoking black holes you'd burn in flesh with a red-hot poker.

He laid a hand on the pink metal casket. Above where the face might be he thought he could detect a faint, humming vibration.

I can't see her, The Jeepster said.

The undertaker cleared his throat. It sounded loud after the utter silence. No, he said. She was injured severely in the face. It's a closed-casket service.

The Jeepster realized he was on the tilted edge of things, where the footing was bad and his grip tenuous at best. He felt the frayed mooring lines that held him part silently and tail away into the dark and he felt a sickening lurch in his very being. There are some places you can't come back from.

He took the pistol out of his waistband. No it's not, he said.

When the three deputies came they came down the embankment past the springhouse into the scrub brush, parting the undergrowth with their heavy, hand-cut snake sticks, and they were the very embodiment of outrage, the bereft father at their fore goading them forward. Righteous anger tricked out in khaki and boots and Sam Browne belts like fate's Gestapo set upon him.

In parodic domesticity he was going up the steps to the abandoned farmhouse with an armful of wood to build a fire for morning coffee. He's leaned the girl against the wall, where she took her ease with her ruined face turned to the dripping trees and the dark fall of her hair drawing off the morning light. The deputies crossed the stream and quickened their pace and come on.

The leaning girl, The Jeepster, the approaching law. These scenes had the sere, charred quality of images unspooling from ancient papyrus or the broken figures crazed on shards of stone pottery.

The Jeepster rose up before them like a wild man, like a beast hounded to its lair. The father struck him in the face and a stick caught him at the base of the neck just above the shoulders and he went down the steps sprawled amid his spilled wood and struggled to his knees. A second blow drove him to his hands, and his palms seemed to be steadying the trembling of the earth itself.

He studied the ground beneath his spread hands. Ants moved among the grass stems like shadowy figures moving between the boles of trees and he saw with unimpeachable clarity that there were other worlds than this one. Worlds layered like the sections of an onion or the pages of a book. He thought he might ease into one of them and be gone, vanish like dew in the hot morning sun.

Then blood gathered on the tip of his nose and dripped and in this heightened reality he could watch the drop descend with infinitesimal slowness and when it finally struck the earth it rang like a hammer on an anvil. The ants tracked it away and abruptly he could see the connections between the worlds, strands of gossamer, sleek and strong as silk.

There are events so terrible in his world their echoes roll world on distant world like ripples on water. Tug a thread and the entire tapestry alters. Pound the walls in one world and in another a portrait falls and shatters.

Goddamn, Cloeave, a voice said. Hold up a minute. I believe you've about to kill him.

When the father's voice came it came from somewhere far above The Jeepster, like the voice of some Old Testament god.

I would kill him if he was worth it but he ain't. A son of a bitch like this just goes through life tearin up stuff, and somebody else has always got to sweep up the glass. He don't know what it is to hurt, he might as well be blind and deaf. He don't feel things the way the rest of us does.

CHARTING THE TERRITORIES OF THE RED

WHEN THE WOMEN CAME BACK from the rest area, slinging their purses along and giggling, Dennis guessed that someone had flirted with them. He hoped they'd keep their mouths shut about it. He was almost certain that Sandy wouldn't say a word, but you never knew about Christy.

Well, we got flirted with, Christy said. She linked an arm through his and leaned against him, standing on his feet, looking up at him. The sun was moving through her auburn hair, and there were already tiny beads of perspiration below her eyes, on the brown, poreless skin of her forehead. She smelled like Juicy Fruit chewing gum.

Dennis unlaced his arm from hers and stepped back and wiped his wire-rimmed glasses on the tail of his shirt. He was wearing jeans and a denim shirt with the sleeves scissored out at the shoulders. He glanced at Wesley. He put the glasses back on and turned and looked at the river. Moving light flashed off it like a heliograph. I guess we need to get the boats in the water, he said.

Wesley had both of Sandy's hands in both of his own. Her hands were small and brown and clasped, so in Wesley's huge fists they looked amputated at the wrists.

Who flirted with you? Wesley asked.

Sandy just grinned and shook her head. She had short dark hair, far shorter than Wesley's. Wesley was looking down into her sharp attentive face. The best thing about her face was her eyes, which large and bluegreen and darkly fringed with thick lashes. The best thing about her eyes was the way they focused on you when you were talking to her, as if she was listening intently and retaining every word. Dennis had always suspected that she did this because she was deaf. Perhaps she didn't even know she did it.

Sandy had once been beaten terribly, but studying her closely Dennis could see no sign of this now. Perhaps the slightest suggestion of aberration about the nose, a hesitant air that she was probably not even aware of. But her skin was clear and brown, the complex and delicate latticework of bones intact beneath it.

Nobody was flirting with us, she said, smiling up at Wesley.

If they did you flashed them a little something, Wesley said.

If I couldn't get flirted with without flashing them a little something I'd just stay at the house, Christy said. She was giggling again. The big one said his name was Lester, she told Wesley. But don't worry, he was ugly and baldheaded.

Lester? What the hell kind of redneck name is Lester? Was he chewing Red Man? Did he have on overalls?

You know, Wesley's not the most sophisticated name I ever heard, Christy said. Nobody's named Wesley, nobody. Do you know one movie star named Wesley?

It occurred to Dennis that Christy might be doing a little flirting herself, although Wesley had been married to Sandy for almost two years and he supposed that he was going to marry Christy himself, someday sooner or later.

I don't know any movie stars named anything at all, Wesley said. I'll make him think goddamn Lester. I'll Lester him.

Wesley wore cutoff jeans and lowcut running shoes with the laces removed. He was bare to the waist and burnt redblack from the sun so he looked like a sinister statuary you'd chopped out of a block of mahogany with a doublebitted axe. He's been in the water, and his jeans were wet, and his hair lay in wet black ringlets.

Nobody was flirting with anybody, Sandy said carefully. She enunciated each word clearly, and Dennis figured this as well was because she had been deaf so long. Now she had an expensive hearing aid smaller than the nail of her little finger, and she could hear as well as anyone, but this had not always been so.

Are you all going to get the boats and stuff? Christy asked.

Let's get everything down from the camp, Dennis said. We can pick the girls up there.

Then let's go, college man, Wesley said.

They followed a black path that wound through wild cane, brambles, blackberry briars. It led to a clearing where they'd spent the night. On the riverbank were sleeping bags and a red plastic ice chest. Dennis began to roll up the sleeping bag he'd slept in with Christy. Sometime far into the night he had awoken, some noise, a nightbird, an owl. Some wild cry that morphed into Sandy's quickened breathing as Wesley made love to her. He wondered if Wesley still beat her. He looped a string round the sleeping bag and lashed it tight. When the breathing had reached some frenzied peak and then slowly subsided to normal, he had turned over, being careful not to wake Christy, and gone back to sleep. He turned now and tossed the sleeping bag into one of the two aluminum canoes tied to a hackberry depending out over the river.

When the canoes rounded the bend through the trailing willow fronds, Dennis saw that a red four-wheel-drive Dodge truck had backed a boat trailer down the sloping bank to the shallows. On it were two aluminum canoes that might have been clones of the ones Dennis and Wesley were rowing. Two men were in the bed of the pickup, two men on the ground. The man unbooming the boats did indeed have on overalls. He was enormous, thicker and heavier than Wesley. He wore the overalls with no shirt, and his head was shaved. The top of his head was starkly white against the sunburned skin of his face, as if he'd just this minute finished shaving it.

Son of a bitch, Wesley said.

This is by God crazy, Dennis said, but Wesley had already drifted the canoe parallel with the shore and was wading out. Don't let this canoe drift into the current, he said over his shoulder. He went up the bank looking at Sandy and Christy. Sandy's face was as blank as a slate you'd erased, but a sort of constrained glee in Christy's told him what he wanted to know. He turned to the men grouped about the red truck.

Lester, I heard you were trying to hit on my wife, he said.

The bald man was turned away, but they were so close Wesley could smell the sweat on him, see the glycerinous drops seeping out of the dark skin of his back. The man had a malignant looking mole the size of a fingertip between his shoulders, where the galluses crossed. The man fitted a key into a lock clasped through two links of chain securing the canoes. The lock popped open, and he freed the chain and locked the hasp through another link and pocketed the key. He turned. He looked up at the two men in the back of the truck and grinned. At last he glanced at Wesley.

The electronic age, he said, and laughed. I reckon it's been all over the news already. He wiped the sweat off his head with a forearm and turned to inspect the women. They'd seated themselves on the bank above, and they were watching like spectators boxseated before some barbaric show.

Which one'd be your wife? Lester asked.

Faced with the prospect of describing his wife or pointing her out like a miscreant in a lineup, Wesley hesitated. Sandy raised her arm. That would be me, she said.

Did I hit on you? Say anything out of the way?

No. You didn't.

The man looked Wesley in the eye. He shrugged. What can I say, he said.

Hey, loosen up, good buddy, one of the men in the truck called. He turned and opened an ice chest and began to remove cans of beer from it. He was bare to the waist, and he had straight, shoulderlength hair that swung with his movement when he turned from the cooler. He tossed a can to Dennis: unprepared, he still caught it onehanded, shifted hands with it. One for the ladies, the man said, and tossed them gently, one, two. When he pitched a fourth to Wesley, Wesley caught it and pivoted and threw it as far as he could out over the river. It vanished without so much as a splash.

Lester looked up at the longhaired man and grinned. Not his brand, he said.

Don't try to bullshit me, Wesley said.

I wouldn't even attempt it, friend, Lester said. He turned to the boat, his back to Wesley, as if he'd simply frozen him out, as if Wesley didn't exist anymore. He unlooped the chain and slid the canoes off the sloped bed into the water. The two men leapt from the bed of the truck and with the third began to load the boats with ice chests, oars, boxes of fishing tackle. They climbed into the canoes and headed them downstream into the current. Lester turned to the women. He doffed an imaginary hat. Ladies, he said.

Wesley seemed to be looking around for a rock to throw.

Let it go, Dennis said.

I could have handled them, Wesley said. All that fine help I had from you.

Dennis turned and spat into the river. Hellfire. You didn't need any help. You made as big a fool of yourself alone as you could have with me helping.

I ain't letting them shitkickers run over me, Wesley said. Hell I got a good Christian raising and a eight-grade education. I don't have to put up with this shit from anybody.

But Wesley's moods were mercurial, and he seemed to find what he had just said amusing. He repeated it to himself, then looked toward the girls. Let's get organized, he said. As soon as Jeeter Lester and his family get gone we'll start looking for that Civil War cave.

He waded out to the canoe containing the red cooler. But first let's all have a little shot of that jet fuel, he said.

Dennis was watching Sandy, and a look like apprehension flickered across her face and was gone. No more than the sudden shadow of a passing cloud. Wesley had removed the lid from the cooler. He had somewhere come by an enormous quantity of tiny bottles of Hiram Walker. They were the kind of bottles served on airlines, and Wesley called them jet fuel. He was fumbling under sandwiches, dumping things out. Jet fuel, jet fuel, he was saying.

I'm sorry, Wesley, Sandy called. I left that bag setting on the kitchen table.

Wesley straightened. Well it'll do a whole hell of a lot of good setting on a table fifty miles from where I am, he said. He sailed the lid out over the river like an enormous rectangular Frisbee.

I said I was sorry. I really am.

Regret is not jet fuel, Wesley said. He hurled the cooler into the water. Everything went: cellophaned sandwiches, a sixpack of Coke, apples bobbing in the rapid current. A bottle of vin rose.

Shit, Dennis said.

Wesley came wading out of the river, Sandy and Christy were buckling on life jackets. Dennis glared sharply at Wesley's face. He stood up and put his folded glasses into the pocket of the denim shirt.

I don't think you're supposed to be throwing crap in the river like that, Christy said.

Oh no, Wesley said. The river police will get me.

Dennis was staring out at the lighthammered water. Lester and his cohorts had drifted out of sight around the bend. Now where is this famous Civil War cave? He asked.

Supposed to be somewheres close, Wesley told him, relaxing visibly. He turned to the women. Can you all handle a canoe?

I can row as good as you can, Christy told him. Maybe better.

You all check out one side of the river and me and this fine defender of southern womanhood'll look on the

other. Check out every bluff, look for anything that might
be a cave. It's supposed to be about halfway up. If you
find a cave, sing out as loud as you can and we'll be there.

OK?

OK.

And keep those life jackets on. If you have to
take a leak or just whatever, do it with the jackets on.

I'm not sure I can do that, Christy said. She
turned and gave Dennis a look so absolutely blank it could
have meant anything. It could have meant, You showed
common sense staying out of that argument he had. Or it
could have meant, Why the hell weren't you backing him
up?

Wesley was looking out across the river.
Goddamn it's hot, he said. Did anybody see where that
beer hit?

They drifted with the current, and Dennis shipped
the oars, only using one occasionally to steer clear of trees
leaning into the water. Huge monoliths of black slate and
pale limestone towered above them, ledges adorned with
dwarf cedars twisted and windformed. The river moved
under them, yellow and murmurous, flexing like the
sleekridged skin of an enormous serpent.

Snipes, Wesley said suddenly.

Dennis thought he meant some kind of bird. He
was scanning the willows and cane. He had a mental
picture of some kind of long legged bird, one foot raised
out of the water, a fish in its mouth.

Where? He asked.

Wesley by God Snipes, Wesley said. Ain't he a movie star?

Yes, he is.

I'll have to tell Christy about that when we catch up. They're done out of sight around that shoal yonder.

After a while Wesley told him again the story of the Civil War cave.

The guy always called it that, the Civil War cave, as if the entire Civil War had been fought inside it. He said it was where Confederate soldiers hid out one time. You can't even see it from the ridge, you have to find it from the river. He said there was all kinds of shit in there. Artifacts. Old guns, lead balls. And bones too, old belt buckles. He didn't even care, can you feature that? Said the guns was all seized up with rust.

In the lifetime he had known Wesley, Dennis had heard this story perhaps a hundred times. He had his mind kicked out of fear, coasting along, listening to the river mumbling to itself. He thought of the look on Sandy's face when Wesley had turned from hurling the cooler into the river, and he thought about gauges.

Once, long ago, on one of the few occasions when he had been blind, falling-down drunk, it had occurred to Dennis that life would be much simpler if everything had a gauge on it, the sort that on an automobile measure the temperature of the engine and so on. If the brain had a gauge you would know immediately how smart a certain decision was. You could start to act on it, keeping an eye on the needle all the time. You could proceed, pull back, try another approach. If the heart had one you'd know how in love you were with somebody. And if you could read their gauge…you could live your life with one eye on the needles and never make a foolish move.

Dennis had made several foolish movements in his life, but he had never wavered in the conviction that Wesley had a gauge in his head. It measured how close he was to violence, and went from zero into uncharted deep red, and every moment of Wesley's life the needle hovered, trembling, on the hairline of white that was all that stood between order and chaos.

Dennis had long ago quit going to bars with Wesley. At a certain point in his drinking, as if a thermostat had clicked on somewhere, Wesley would swivel his stool and survey the room with a smile of good-natured benevolence, studying its contents as if to ascertain were there inanimate objects worth breaking, folks worth putting in the hospital.

Six months after he married Sandy, he had eased into the bedroom of an apartment in the housing project and studied the sleeping faces of Sandy and a man named Bobby Joe Seales. He had slammed Seales full in the face with his fist, then turned his attention to Sandy. He had broken her arm and nose and jaw and shifted back to Seales. The room was a scene of carnage, folks said, blood on the floor, blood on the walls, blood on the ceiling. He had ripped the shade from a lamp and used the lamp base as a club, beating Seales viciously. Folks came screaming, cops. Dennis did not hear this story from Wesley, or from Sandy, but he had heard it plenty of other places, and Wesley stood trial for aggravated assault. The son of a bitch aggravated me, Wesley had said. So I assaulted him.

Seals had been on the Critical List. Folks always spoke of it in capital letters as if it were a place. A place you didn't want to go. Don't fuck with Wesley Deavers, Folks said. He put Bobby Joe Scales on the Critical List. It looked like they'd been killing hogs in there.

Did you hear something?

Dennis listened. All he could hear was the river, crows spilling raucous cries from above them, doves mourning from some deep hollow he couldn't see.

Something. Sounded like yelling.

Then he could hear voices, faint at first, sourceless, as if they were coming from thin air, or out of the depths of the yellow water. Then he heard, faint and faint: Dennis. Dennis.

They've found it. Wesley said. He took up his oars and turned the boat into the swift current. Let's move it, he said. The voices had grown louder. If this is the right cave we'll map it, Wesley said. Make us up some charts so we can find it again.

The river widened where it shoaled, then began narrowing into a bottleneck as the bend came up. Dennis could feel the river quickening under him, the canoe gaining urgency as it rocked in the current.

Dennis. Dennis.

I wish she'd shut the hell up, Dennis said.

All right, all right, Wesley yelled. We're coming.

That must be one hellacious cave.

But the cliffs had been tending away for some time now on this side of the river, and when they rounded the bend they saw that the bluffs had subsided to a steep, stony embankment where Christy and Sandy were huddled. Dennis couldn't see their canoe. They were on their knees and still wearing life jackets, their hair plastered tightly to their skulls. Sandy was crying, and Christy was talking to her and had an arm about her shoulders.

Now what the fuck is this news, Wesley said, and Dennis felt a cold shudder of unease. He remembered something Dorothy Parker had purportedly said once when her doorbell rang: What fresh hell is this?

They tipped us over, Christy said. Now she began to cry as well. Goddamn them. They were waiting for us here and grabbed the boat. All four of them, two boatloads. They tried to get us into the boats with them and when we wouldn't go they got rough, tried to drag us. I hit one with an oar, and that baldheaded fucker tipped us over. They took the boat.

Wesley seemed actually to pale. Dennis could see a cold pallor beneath the deep tan. It seemed to pulse in his face. Sandy, are you all right? Wesley asked.

She can't hear, Christy said. When we went under it did something to her hearing aid, ruined it. Shorted it out or something. She can't hear a thing. I mean not a goddamned thing.

Oh, Wesley cried. He seemed on the threshold of a seizure, some sort of rage induced attack. Eight hundred fucking dollars, he said. Eight hundred dollars up a wild hog's ass and gone. I'm going to kill them. I'm going to absolutely fucking kill them.

Wesley made twelve dollars an hour, and Dennis knew that he was mentally dividing twelve into eight hundred and arriving at the number of hours he had worked to pay for the hearing aid.

Where's the other oars?

I don't know. They floated off.

I'm gone. I'm going to kill them graveyard dead.

He turned the boat about to face the current.

Hey, Christy called. Wait.

Stay right here, Wesley said. And I mean right here. Do not move from that rock till we get back with the boat.

Let them keep the goddamned boat, Christy screamed, but Wesley didn't reply. He heeled into the current and began to row. He did not speak for a long time. He rowed like a madman, like some sort of rowing machine kicked up on high. I'll row when you get tired, Dennis said. Fuck that, Wesley told him. After a while he looked back and grinned. How dead am I going to kill them? He asked.

Graveyard dead, Dennis said.

Wesley hadn't missed a stroke rowing. After a time he said, There will be some slow riding and sad singing.

Trees went by on the twin shorelines like a landscape unspooling endlessly from one reel to another. A flock of birds went down the metallic sky like a handful of hurled slate. Dennis guessed the Lester gang was long gone, into the tall timber, their canoes hidden in the brush, laughing and drinking beer, on their way back across the ridges to pick up their truck.

What were you going to do, back there, kick my ass?

Dennis was looking at the sliding yellow water. What?

Back there at the camp when my jet fuel was missing. You got up and folded your little glasses and shoved them in your pocket. You looked for all the world like a schoolteacher getting ready to straighten some folks out. You think you can kick my ass?

I wouldn't want to hurt you, Dennis said.

Wesley laughed. How long have you known me, Dennis?

You know that. Since the third grade.

Third grade. Have I ever lied to you?

I don't know. How would I know that? Not that I know of.

I never lied to you. So I'm telling the truth now. I'm going to kill them. I'm going to kill them with an oar, not flat like I was paddling their ass, but sideways like I was chopping wood. I'll take their heads off. Do you want out? I'll ease over and let you out.

The boat hadn't slackened. The oars dipped and pulled, dipped and pulled, with no variation in their rhythm. The boat seemed to have attained its own volition, its own momentum.

No, Dennis finally said, and he knew with a cold horror that Wesley was telling the truth.

Do you really think I'd stop long enough to let you out?

You never lie.

No.

I can ask you the one right question and you'll lie.

Ask it then.

But before he could ask it, Wesley suddenly shouted. A hoarse cry of exultation. Dennis looked. They were aligned on a sandbar far downriver, three of them, the three canoes beached on the shore like bright metallic whales. Tiny dark figures in attitudes of waiting, watching them come.

Shouts came skipping across the water. Now he could see that Lester had his hands cupped about his mouth like a megaphone. It took you long enough, he yelled.

Wesley might not have heard. He was leaning into the oars, the muscles in the arms that worked them knotting and relaxing, knotting and relaxing.

They stood like the last ragged phalanx of an army backed to the last wall there was. They each held an oar. When the boat was still twenty feet from the shoreline Wesley bailed out. Oar aloft like God's swift sword. He seemed to be skimming the surface, a dark, vengeful divinity the waters would not even have. He knocked Lester's oar aside with his own and drew back and swung. The oar made an eerie, abrupt whistling. Blood misted the air like paint from an exploding spray can. Lester went to his knees clutching his face, blood streaming between his fingers. Wesley hit him across the top of the head, and a vulval gash opened in the shaven flesh. Dennis slammed the longhaired man backward, and he stumbled and fell into a thicket of willows and wild cane. He advanced on him, swinging the oar like a man killing snakes. An oar caught him across the bicep, and his left arm went suddenly numb. He turned. A man with a fright wig of wild red hair and clenched yellow teeth broadsided him in the shoulder with the flat of an oar just as Wesley broke his own oar across the man's back. Wesley was left with a section half the length of a baseball bat. The redhaired man was going to run through the cane, and Wesley threw the stub of the paddle at him.

The longhaired man had simply vanished. Dennis had driven him into the cane, and he'd just disappeared. Dennis was almost giddy with relief. It seemed over before it had properly begun, and it had not been as bad as he had feared it would be.

Lester was crawling on his hands and knees away from the river. He crawled blindly, his eyes full of blood, which dripped into the sand below him.

Wesley picked up a discarded oar and walked between Lester and the growth of willows. He had the oar cocked like a chopping ax. Lester crawled on. When his head bumped Wesley's knee he reared backward, sitting on his folded legs. He made a mute, armsspread gesture of supplication.

Wesley, Dennis yelled.

Kill this motherfucker graveyard dead, Wesley said.

Dennis crossed the sand in two long strides and swung onto Wesley's arm and wrested the oar from him. Wesley sat down hard in the sand. He got up shaking his head as if he'd clear it. He crossed the sandbar and waded kneedeep into the river and scooped up handfuls of water and washed his face. Lester crawled on. Like something wounded that just won't die. When he was into the willows he struggled up and stood leaning with both hands cupping his knees. Then he straightened and began wiping the blood out of his eyes. Dennis lay on his back in the sand for a long time and stared into the sky, studying the shifting patterns the clouds made. Both arms ached, and he was slowly clasping and unclasping his left hand. The bowl of the sky spun slowly clockwise, like pale blue water emptying down an endless drain.

He could hear Lester lumbering off through the brush. Wesley came up and dropped onto the sand beside Dennis. Dennis had an arm flung across his eyes. He thought he might just lie here in the hot weight of the sun forever. His ribs hurt, and he could feel his muscles beginning to stiffen.

I wish I hadn't quit smoking and I had a cigarette, Wesley said. Or maybe a little shot of that jet fuel. Chastising rednecks is hot, heavy work, and it does wear a man out so.

Dennis didn't reply, and after a time Wesley said, You ought to've let me kill him. I knew you weren't as committed as I was. I could see your heart wasn't in it. You didn't have your mind right.

He was dragging off like a snake with its back broke, Dennis said. What the hell do you want? Let it be.

We need to get these boats back to where Sandy and Christy are. Damned if I don't dread rowing upstream. Bad as I feel. You reckon we could rig up a towline and pull them along the bank?

I don't know.

You don't think they'd go back to where the girls are, do you?

I don't know.

We better go see. No telling what kind of depravities those inbred mutants could think of to do with an innocent young girl.

Dennis suddenly dropped the arm from his eyes and sat up. He could hear a truck engine. It was in the distance, but approaching, and the engine sounded wound out, as if it were being rawhided over and through the brush. He stood up. The truck seemed to be coming through the timber, and he realized that a road, probably an unused and grownover logging road, ran parallel with the river. They know this river, he thought. The fourth man went to get the truck. Through a break in the trees chrome mirrored back the light, the sun hammered off bright red metal. The truck stopped. The engine died. Immediately Dennis could hear voices, by turns angry and placating. They seemed to be fighting amongst themselves, trying to talk Lester either into or out of doing something. A door slammed, another or the same door slammed again. When he looked around, Wesley had risen and gathered up two of the paddles. He reached one of them to Dennis. Dennis waved it away. Let's get the hell out of Dodge, he said.

We got to get the boats.

To hell with the boats. We got to move.

Something was coming through the brake of wild cane, not walking or even running as a man might, but lurching and stumbling and crashing, some beast enraged past reason, past pain. Wesley turned toward the noise and waited with the oar at a loose port arms across his chest.

Lester came out of the cane with a .357 Magnum clasped bothhanded before him. It looked enormous even in his huge hands. Lester looked like something that had escaped halfbutchered from a meatpacker's clutches, like some bloody experiment gone awry. His wild eyes were just black holes charred in the bloody suet of his face. The bullet splintered the oar and slammed into Wesley's chest. Wesley's head, his feet, seemed to jerk forward. Then Lester shot him in the head, and Wesley sprang backward as if a spingloaded tether had jerked him away.

Dennis was at the edge of the canebrake running full out. He glanced back. The pistol swung around. He dove sideways into the cane, rolling, and running from the ground up as the explosion showered him with sand, the cane tilting and swaying in his bobbing vision. The horizon jerked with his footfalls. Another shot, shouts, curses, men running down from the truck. He'd lost his glasses, and trees swam into his blurred vision as though surfacing at breakneck speed from murky water. Branches clawed at him, a lowhanging vine hurled him forward like a projectile blown out of the wall of greenery. He slowed and went on. He could hear excited voices, but nobody seemed to be pursuing him. He went on anyway, his lungs hot as if he moved through a medium of smoke, of pure fire. The timber deepened, and he went on into it. He fell and lay across the roots of an enormous beech. The earth was loamy and black and smelled like corrupting flesh. He vomited and lay with his face in the vomit. He closed his eyes. After a while the truck cranked and retreated the way it had come, fast, winding out. He raised his face and spat. There was a taste in his mouth like a cankered penny, and he could smell fear on himself like an animal's rank musk that you can't wash off.

When he finally made it back to the sandbar, the first thing he did was hunt his glasses. They were lying in the cane where he'd dived and rolled, and earpiece bent at a crazy angle but nothing broken. He put them on, and everything jerked into focus, as if a vibratory world had abruptly halted its motion.

Wesley was on his back with the back of his head and both hands lying in the water. He looked as if he'd flung his arms up in surrender, way too late. Dennis looked away. He took off the denim shirt and spread it across Wesley's face.

He dragged one of the canoes parallel with the body and began trying to roll Wesley into it. Wesley was a big man, and this was no easy task. He was loath to touch the bare flesh, but finally there was no way round it and he picked up the legs and worked them across the canoe and braced his feet and tugged the torso over into it.

The boat lurched in the shallow water. By this time he was crying, making animal sounds he did not recognize as coming from himself. He threw in two oars and, running behind the boat, shoved it into deeper water. When he climbed in, he had to sit with a foot on either side of Wesley's thighs in order to row. In the west the sinking sun was burning through the trees with a bluegold light.

Twilight was falling when he came upon them, a quarter mile or so downriver from where they'd been left. They were straggling along the bank, Christy carrying what he guessed was a stick for cottonmouths. He oared the boat around broadside and rowed to shore. He waded the last few feet and dragged the prow into the bank, turned toward the women. They were looking not at him but at what was in the boat. All this time he'd been wondering what he could say to Sandy, but he remembered with dizzy relief that she was deaf and he wouldn't have to say anything at all. There didn't seem to be any questions anyway, or any answers worth giving if there were.

Christy's face was a twisted gargoyle's mask. Oh no, she said. Oh, Jesus, please no.

Dennis sat on the bank with his feet in the water. Rowing upstream had been hard, and he had his bloody palms upturned on his knees, studying the broken blisters. Sandy rose and climbed down the embankment, steadying her descent with a hand on Dennis's shoulder. She stood staring down into the boat. She knelt in the shallow water. Dennis stood up and waded around the boat and steadied it. He looked curiously like a salesman standing at the ready to demonstrate something should the need arise. He could hear Christy crying. She cried on and on.

Wesley lay with the bloody shirt still flung across his face. He lay like a fallen giant. Treetrunk legs, huge bronze torso. Sandy took up one of his hands and held it. The great fingers, thick black hair between the knuckles. She held the hand a time, and then she began folding the limp fingers into a fist, a finger at a time, tucking the thumb down and holding the hand in a fist with her own two hands. She sat and looked at it. Dennis suddenly wondered if she was seeing the fist come at her out of a bloody and abrupt awakening, rising and falling as remorselessly as a knacker's hammer, and he leaned and disengaged her hand. The loose fist slapped against the hull and lay palm upward.

He thought she might be crying, but when he looked up her eyes were dry and calm. They locked with his. Nor would she look away, as if she were waiting for his lips to move so she could read them.

We've got to get him out of here, Christy sobbed. A road somewhere maybe, somebody would stop.

Nobody answered her. Dennis wasn't listening, and Sandy couldn't hear at all. He wondered what it would sound like to be deaf. What you'd hear. From the look on Sandy's face across the body of her fallen warrior he judged it must be a calm and restful sound, the sighing of a perpetual wind through clashing rushes, a lapping of peaceful water that never varies or ceases.

Time Done Been Won't Be No More

EXCERPT FROM THE LOST COUNTRY

THE COURT HAD AWARDED HER custody of the motorcycle, they were going this day to get it. Edgewater was sitting on the curb drinking orange juice from a cardboard carton when the white Ford convertible came around the corner. A Crown Victoria with the top down though the day was cool and Edgewater had been sitting in the sun for such heat as there was. The car was towing what he judged to be a horse trailer.

Claire eased the car to the curb and shoved it into park and left it idling. She was wearing a scarf over her dirty blonde hair and an air vaguely theatrical and when she pushed her sunglasses up with a scarlet fingernail her eyes were the color of irises.

What are you doing in this part of town, Sailor?

Just waiting for someone like you to come along, he said.

You ready to roll?

He got in and slammed the door. Ready as I'll ever be.

This was Memphis Tennessee, the middle of April in 1952, the convertible already rolling, washed-out sunlight running on the storefront glass like luminous water. She was driving down a series of side streets into a steadily degenerating neighborhood. Where winos and such streetfolk as were yet about seemed stunned by this regenerative sun and so unaccustomed to such an abundance of light that they drifted alleyward as if extended exposure might scorch them or sear away their clothing. Bars and liquor stores contested for space on these narrow streets and both seemed well represented. They had a stunned vacuous look to them and their scrollworks of dead neon waited for nightfall.

She glanced across at him.

God I hate the way you dress, she said. I'm going to have to buy you some clothes.

Edgewater was wearing a Navy dungaree shirt and jeans held up by a webbed belt the buckle of which proclaimed US Navy. I'm all right, he said.

Listen. You're going to have to bear with me on this. Just hang in there no matter what happens, okay?

Wait a minute. What does that mean, no matter what happens? I thought we were just picking up your motorcycle.

Well, you know. They were my in-laws, after all. There might be a few hard feelings.

Here were paintlorn Victorian mansions where nothing remained of opulence save a faint memory. Rattletrap cars convalescing or dying beneath lowering elms. Shadetree mechanics stared into their motors as if they'd resuscitate them by sheer will or raise them from the dead with the electric hands of faithhealers.

Past a rotting blue mansion with a red tiled roof she halted the car and peering backward with a cigarette cocked in the corner of her mouth she cut the wheel and backed the trailer expertly over the sidewalk and down a driveway bowered by lowhanging willows.

Showtime, she said.

All polished chrome and sleek black leather the motorcycle seemed waiting and coiled to spring, setting alien and futuristic in the back yard.

Claire got out and slammed the door. Edgewater followed, climbing slowly out of the car like someone cautiously easing into deep cold waters. There were a couple of two-by-eights in the bed of the trailer and he aligned them into a makeshift ramp and turned to the Harley Davidson leaning on its kickstand.

A screen door slapped loosely against its frame. A short heavyset woman had come onto the back porch and she was crossing the porch rapidly in no nonsense strides and she was rubbing her hands together in an anticipatory way. Put one whore's hand on that motorcycle and you'll pull back a bloody stub, she said.

Hurry, Claire said.

He'd no more than raised the kickstand and angled the front wheel toward the ramp when the woman began to scream. You ruined my son's life, you bitch, she yelled. She was coming down the steps two at a time and Claire turned and took a tentative step away but the woman closed on her remorseless and implacable as a stormfront and slapped her face hard then laid a hand to each of Claire's shoulders and flung her onto the grass and fell upon her.

Shit, Edgewater said.

He had the motorcycle halfway up the ramp when the screen door slapped again and a man with a torn gray undershirt came out with a doublebarreled shotgun unbreeched and he was fumbling waxed red cylinders into it. He dropped one and was feeling wildly about the floor for it.

By the time Edgewater heard the gun barrel slap up he'd rolled the cycle off the ramp and straddled it and kickstarted it and he was already rolling when the concussion came like a slap to the head. He went through shredded greenery that spun like windy green snow, skidding blindly onto the street then across it and through a hedge before he could get the motorcycle under control and out onto the street again, leaning into the wind and houses kaleidoscoping past on either side like the walls of a gaudy tunnel he was catapulted through.

The imaged street rolled in and out of the rearview mirror then the white Ford appeared and followed at a sedate pace. Edgewater slowed and turned the motorcycle into the parking lot of a liquor store and she turned in beside it. The Harley idled like some fierce beast that wasn't even breathing hard. She was laughing.

Hard feelings my ass, Edgewater said.

Do you believe this? My brother-in-law had to run out and wrestle him for the gun. He shot the shit out of that tree, did you see that?

I rode through it, Edgewater said.

Ahh baby you got it all in your hair, she said, brushing it away with a hand.

They had to manhandle the cycle onto the trailer because she hadn't thought it wise to stop for the boards and Edgewater lashed it upright to a support with the rope she'd brought.

That's twice I've wrestled this heavy son of a bitch up here, he said. My first time and my last.

You're in a good mood, she said, grinning, getting into the car.

I'm not real fond of getting shot at, Edgewater said.

She eased the car out into the street and headed north, glancing in the rearview mirror to check was the cycle secure. You'll feel better tonight, she said. We'll get you a sport coat somewhere and go out to a really good restaurant. Italian maybe, we'll get a nice bottle of wine. Okay?

Okay, Edgewater said.

The prospective motorcycle buyer lived in a town called Leighton east of Memphis and they drove toward it past tract houses and apartment complexes and onto a flat countryside of housetrailers and farmland beset by tractors that Edgewater watched move silent down cottonfields that seemed endless.

He turned to study her against the slipsliding landscape. There was a faint blue bruise at the corner of her right eye and a scratch on her cheek but with the wind blowing her hair and the silk scarf strung out in the breeze she looked rakish and well satisfied with herself. In the brief time he'd known her she seemed always to be playing some role. Seldom the same one twice. Just the star of whatever movie today was. He'd had the impulse to glance about and see whether cinecameras were whirring away, a makeup man with his potions at the ready.

Then as he watched her profile seemed to alter. The flesh itself to sear and melt and run off the skull and cascade down the linen blouse she wore and the linen itself blackened and rotted and the wind sucked tatters of it away and when she turned to grin at him bone hand clutching the steering wheel the hollow eyesockets of her skull smoked like a charred landscape beyond which a faint yellow light flickered and died. Her grinning teeth had loosened in their sockets and there was a blackened cavity where the right canine joined the jawbone.

They were coming up on a white stucco building with a Falstaff beer sign framed by a rectangle of light bulbs. Carolyn's Place, the sign said.

Pull in there, Edgewater said.

What?

Let me wait here for you. I have to make a phone call.

She'd already begun to slow but she turned to frown at him. This doesn't make any sense, she said. We're almost to Leighton. You can call from there. Besides, who would you call? You don't know anybody.

He was out almost before the car stopped rolling. Pick me up after you get your business transacted. I'll be in there drinking a beer.

She glanced toward the sign. Just make damn sure you keep your hands off Carolyn, she said.

Edgewater crossed a glaring white parking lot of crushed mussel shells. Carolyn's Place was set on earth so absolutely bare of tree and shrub that the stuccoed honky-tonk seemed to have sucked up all the nourishment for miles around. Dancing Saturday night to live music, a placard in the window promised, but Edgewater was already touched by a rising desperation and he promised himself that by Saturday night he'd be dancing somewhere else.

He went into a cool gloom that smelled of hops and cigarette smoke and all seemed touched by a silence so dense it was almost cloistral. A man seated at the bar watched him cross the room. Edgewater's eyes were still full of the April light from outside and the room seemed a cave he was walking into, the drinkers seated at the tables troglodytes who'd laid aside momentarily their picks and were taking respite from their labors.

Let me have a draft, he told the barkeep. He withdrew a worn and folded five dollar bill from the watchpocket of his jeans. The barkeep filled a frosted mug from a tap and raked the foam into a slotted trough and slid the beer across the counter. The barkeep had vaselined red hair parted in the middle and a red freckled face and brownspotted fingers like sausages.

Edgewater took a long pull from the beer and lit a cigarette and sat just enjoying the silence. Even the drinkers at the tables were quiet, as if still contemplative of whatever had befallen them the night before. He could feel the silence like a comforter he'd drawn about him and he was glad that Claire and the motorcycle were rolling somewhere away from him.

There was something jittery about Claire that precluded calm. She was always in motion and always talking. He'd watched her sleep and even then her life went on, her face jerking in nervous tics at the side of her mouth, her iriscolored eyes moving beneath nightranslucent lids like swift blue waters. Her limbs stirred restlessly and he'd decided even her dreams were brighter and louder and faster than those allotted the rest of the world. Watching her sleep he felt he'd stolen something he did not want but nevertheless could not be returned.

He felt eyes upon him and looked up. The man two stools downbar was watching him. He was a heavyset man in overalls whose tiny piglike eyes were studying Edgewater in drunken fixation. He seemed to be trying to remember where he'd seen Edgewater or perhaps someone like him. He made some gesture near indecipherable to the barkeep and the barkeep brought up from the cooler a dripping brown bottle and opened it and set it before the man then refilled his shotglass with something akin to ceremony.

What are you lookin at? the man asked Edgewater.

Nothing, Edgewater said. He looked away, to the mirror behind the aligned green bottles. His reflection dark and thin and twisted in the wonky glass.

He took up three of the dollar bills and slid them across the bar. Let me have some change for the telephone, he said.

Was you in the war? The man downbar asked him.

Edgewater thought of the concussion of the shotgun, the drifting shreds of willow leaves. Not in one of the official ones, he said.

Change rattled on the bar.

What the hell's that supposed to mean?

He raked the change and cupping it in a palm went past a silent jukebox to the rear wall where a telephone hung. He stood watching it for a time as if puzzled by its function or manner of operation, the fisted change heavy in his hand and he could feel sweat in his armpits tracking coldly down his ribcage. He turned and went through a door marked MEN and urinated in a discolored trough and washed his hands and face at the sink and toweled dry on a length of fabric he unreeled from its metal container. Above the sink there was no mirror, just four brackets where a mirror had been. On the spackled plaster some wag with a black marker had written, you look just fine.

He went out and used the phone, heard it ring in what by now seemed some other world entire. Yet the room where the phone rang and rang was real in his mind and he wondered idly was anything missing, anything added, had they painted the living room walls.

Finally a young woman answered the phone. Edgewater's sister.

I'd about give up on you, Edgewater said.

Billy? Is that you? Where in the world are you at? How is he?

He's how I said he was the last time you called. He's dying. Why ain't you here?

I'm on the way, he said. I'll be there. I ran into a little bad luck.

She knew him, she didn't even want details. You'd better get here, she said. He has to see you. Has to. He wants to make it right. He's tryin to hang on until you get here.

He said that? He said he's trying to hang on until I get there?

You know some things without them bein said, she told him. Or ought to. Would you want to go before your maker carryin all that?

I'm not looking forward to it carrying it or emptyhanded either, Edgewater said.

Well. You and your smart mouth.

I've got to go, Edgewater said.

There's something wrong with you, she said. If you weren't so–

He quietly broke the connection and cradled the phone. Then he took it up again and held it to his ear and it seemed a wonder that there was only the dialtone. No news good or bad, just a monotonous onenote electrical drone, sourceless yet all around him, the eternal hum of whatever powers the world, slowly diminishing. He recradled the phone.

The man at the bar had swiveled his stool to watch Edgewater and Edgewater had seen the look on his face on other faces and he thought, Fuck this. He picked up his beer and what remained of his change and moved to the corner of the bar.

You're out of uniform, the man called after him.

I'm discharged, Edgewater said. I'm not in the service.

The man struggled off the stool and drained the shotglass and turned up his chaser and drank, adam's apple pumping spasmodically. He set the bottle back and lumbered heavily toward Edgewater like a gracelorn dancing bear. Edgewater wished for a pool cue, magic winged shoes. A motorcycle.

You disrespectin that uniform whether you in or out. Them's Navy workclothes, don't think I don't recognize them. What I wore all durin the war. You got on them clothes and you're not even covered.

I got discharged, Edgewater said carefully, straining for clarity. In Long Beach, California. I'm out. I served four years and I'm on my way home.

He picked up his mug and cigarettes. He pocketed the Luckies and moved farther up the bar. Let me have another draft, he said.

Don't fuck with Ed, the barkeep said. He's bad news.

He damn sure is, Edgewater said. But I'm hoping it's for somebody else.

How about you fuckers? The man asked. He'd approached again and was leaning forward into

Edgewater's face. Edgewater could smell him, see the cratered pores of his skin, veins like tiny exploded faultlines in his nose, feel his angry pyorrheic breath.

While I was over there across the waters fightin and dyin you fuckers was over here drinkin all our whiskey and screwin our wives. What about that?

Hellfire, Edgewater said. I wasn't even old enough for that war. How about leavin me the hell alone?

Fought and died for you fuckers. Got medals to prove it.

How about that beer, Edgewater said.

Maybe you ought to just to drink up and move along, the barkeep said. His head gleamed like a metallic cap. You're not a regular customer.

I might become one, Edgewater said.

Then again you might not.

You was probably one of them, one of them conscious objectors, Ed said.

Edgewater drained the mug and set it gently atop the bar. He turned to go but before he'd taken the first step a heavy hand fixed on his shirt collar and jerked hard and he felt the buttons pop away and the shirt rip down the back. It all happened very quickly. He whirled and grasped the mug and slammed Ed in the side of the head with it. It didn't even break and while he was looking at it in a sort of wonder the barkeep disdaining normal means of approach vaulted the bar with a weighted length of sawnoff pool cue and slapped Edgewater hard above the left ear. Edgewater's knees went to water and he pooled on the floor. The world went light then dark. Somebody

kicked him in the side and a wave of nausea rocked him. His vision darkened gray to black and after a while when he came to he could hear sirens. The old man is finally dead and here comes the ambulance, he thought. He looked about. Ed was at the bar downing a shot and the barkeep was at his station and the troglodytes seemed not to have glanced up. Whoop whoop whoop the siren went.
A wave of vomit lapped at his feet. Edgewater spat blood and pillowed his head on his arm and closed his eyes.

They came out of the city hall in Leighton and down the steps into the sunlight. The Crown Victoria waited at a parking meter and he got in and closed the door. It was a while before Claire got in. She stood by the car peering in at him, studying him as if he was something malignant, bad news on a glass slide. Finally she got in. Her jaws were tightened and muscles worked there and she clutched the purse as if it were some weapon she might fall upon him with.

But the sun was warm and Edgewater closed his eyes and turned his bruised face to it and just absorbed that and the heat from the hot plastic behind his head.

He could hear her fumbling out the keys. The engine cranked and they were in motion. They rode for a time in silence.

What do you have to say for yourself? She finally asked.

He opened his eyes. Not much, he said.

You son of a bitch. How do you plan on paying this money back? That was a big chunk of my motorcycle money.

He didn't say anything.

You beat anything I ever saw.

Edgewater dug out the crumpled pack of Lucky Strikes the jailer had returned to him. He pulled one out and straightened it and lit it from the dash lighter. He turned and watched the sliding landscape. He didn't know where they were going but the countryside was slipping away, field and stone and fence, cows like tiny painted cows in a proletariat mural. A dreadful flat sameness to this western world. It went rolling away to where the blue horizon and bluer sky were demarcated by windrowed reefs of salmoncolored clouds.

You wouldn't even have called me. I had to go looking for you in that terrible bar and hear about you picking a fight with some war veteran. What's the matter with you? I should have just let you rot there.

He seemed not to have heard. Beyond the windowglass a man clutching the handles of a turning plow went down a black field so distant he seemed in some illusory manner to be pushing plow and mules before him. Edgewater wondered what his life was like. What his wife said to him when he came in from the fields, what they talked about across the supper table. He would have two children, a boy and a girl. Later he would tell them a story as their eyelids grew heavy and sleep eddied about them like encroaching waters. A flock of blackbirds tilted and cartwheeled and spun like random debris the wind was driving before it.

I know as well as anything you did it deliberately. Set this whole thing up. You couldn't just walk away like anybody else. You have to get yourself locked up and ruin the nice dinner plans I had made and waste all that money.

Is there much more of this? he asked.

I've just about had it with you. And on top of everything else you're the coldest human being I've ever seen. And I've seen some cold ones.

I'll get out anywhere along here, Edgewater said.

What?

Let me out of the car.

She locked the brakes and the car slid to the shoulder of the road and set rocking on its shocks. Edgewater got out. A car was approached behind them. He turned and stuck out a thumb. In the sun the car seemed to be warping up out of the blacktop road itself, swift and gleaming and shifting through transient stages as if it had not yet assumed its true form. It shot by without slowing in a wake of dust and roadside paper that rose and subsided furtively to earth. He went on. After a time she put the Ford in gear and followed along beside him until he went down the embankment and climbed through a barbedwire fence and started across the field. She stopped the car then and shouted at him then gathered an armful of stones and began to hurl them at him. But her arm was poor and the stones fell wide as did the curses she cast that in the end were just words and he had heard them all so often they had become powerless.

He went on.

Night. Cold vapors swirled the earth like groundfog. Midnight maybe, perhaps later, it scarcely seemed to matter. The last ride had let him out on this road hours ago and he walked through a country which in these shuttered hours seemed uninhabited. Not even a dog barked. Just a steady cacophony of insects from the woods that fell silent at his approach and rose again with his passage, an owl from some timbered hollow so distant he might have dreamed it. Nothing on this road and he thought he'd taken a wrong turn but then it occurred to him that on a journey such as this there are no wrong turns. If all destinations are one it matters little which road you take. The pale road was awash with moonlight as far as he could see and in these clockless hours when the edges of things blur and the mind tugs gently at its moorings it seemed to him that the road had never been traversed before and once his footfalls honed away faint and fainter to ultimate nothingness it would never be used again.

The moon rose, ascended through curdled clouds of silver and violet. His shadow appeared, long and ungainly, jerked along on invisible wires, a misbegotten familiar he was following down this moonlit road.

It had grown cold with the fall of night and he thought with regret of his coat and blanket at Claire's apartment but there was nothing for that. He looked both up and down the empty road but source and destination faded into the same still silver mist. He left the road and angled cautiously through branches and blackberry briars into the woods.

The passage of an hour had him before a huge bonfire, the piles of leached stumps and deadfall branches and uprooted cedar fenceposts with stubs of wire still appended roaring like a freight train and sparks and flaming leaves cascading upward in a funnel of pure heat.

He warmed awhile then seated himself on a length of log and unpocketed and unwrapped a candy bar and ate it in tiny bites, forcing himself to chew slowly, making it last. There were two cigarettes remaining in the pack and he lit one and tucked the other carefully aside for the morning. When he'd finished the cigarette he built up the fire and lay down with the log for a pillow.

Out of the dark a whippoorwill called three times and ceased, whippoorwill, whippoorwill, whippoorwill. After a time another called from a distant part of the wood but the first remained silent, as if he'd said all there was to say. Edgewater closed his eyes and for a time images of the day lost drifted through his mind like a disjointed film he was watching. Slowly he settled into sleep.

His dreams were troubled and he tried to wake but could not. In the dream he was in a Mexican hotel room. There was a bed, a basin, a chest of drawers. From rooms up and down the hall came shouts and raucous laughter but no one was laughing here. Here something had gone awry.

The girl on the bed was leaking. Spreadeagled on spreading scarlet as if her white body lay on an enormous American Beauty rose that grew as malign and ill-formed as cancer. The old woman and her smocked assistant were preparing to flee. Rats who'd choose any ship but this one. The woman said something in Spanish he didn't understand and the man mimicked her hasty exit and left the door ajar and before he fled himself he leaned closely into her face and watched the fluttering of her eyelids and cupped his hand hard between her legs as if he'd contain her and don't, he said, don't, as if dying was a matter you had any say in.

He wanted out of the room and out of this dream and he went down the hall opening doors upon startled participants in their various couplings and a girl on hands and knees being mounted by her lover like a dog turned and studied him calmly over her shoulder with breasts pendulumed between her distended arms and her hair falling like a black waterfall and as her lover slid into her she looked away and Edgewater closed the door. In the room next a sailor was emptying a bottle of Rose hair oil into the graythatched vagina of an old woman and in the next a man turned to blow out the match he'd fired the window curtains with and he grinned at Edgewater and winked while behind him the gauzy curtains climbed the walls like flaming morninglories and the rosedappled wallpaper curled and smoked and stank like burning flesh.

His father and his sister were in the next room, the old man abed and the sister attendant. His caved face, his deathroom smell. The eyes of some old predator who's crawled into his den to die. She turned from her ministering with a damp cloth in her hand and Edgewater saw that the old man had been berating her and she was crying. She dropped the cloth, she turned away and leaned against the plaster. Undone, she wept against limegreen walls. Finally she turned upon her brother such a look of sadness and loss that he wept despite himself. If you weren't so, she said, and he closed the door in her face.

Before the last door he stood holding the last doorknob. It was hot to the touch and seemed to vibrate beneath his fingers and something was holding it on the other side of the door. He realized that beyond this door lay whatever the other rooms had been preparing him for. He steeled his nerve and took a deep breath of the smoky air and twisted the doorknob hard and shoved the door open and fell into the room.

He woke shaking and appalled and for a moment he didn't know where he was, where he'd been. He wiped a hand across his mouth. He held his face in his palms. God, he said. God. He raised his face and hugged himself against the cold. The fire had burned to a feathery white ash that rose and drifted in what breeze there was and there was a steely quality to the bluegray light that stood between the trees.

Objects were softly emergent, tree and stump and mossgrown stone, and to Edgewater these objects seemed to be attaining not mere visibility but existence, things that were being born into the world for the first time before his eyes and he studied these things in a kind of bemused wonder.

He had a thought toward rebuilding the fire but more than warmth he wanted quit of this glade of dreams and he paused only long enough to rake the ash away until he found a glowing coal to light his cigarette.

When he came out of the woods onto the roadbed there was already a faint roseate glow in the east and he went on toward it through the first tentative birdsongs. The world was awakening. All sounds were clear and equidistant, somewhere a cock heralded the dawn, on some unseen road a laboring truck shifted gears. A red rim of sun crept above the trees and consumed the horizon with gold and silver light.

Hunger lay in his stomach like a fistsize chunk of teeth and claws and broken bones but his heart was lifting and his feet felt fleet and light. The day was new and unused and this day was one that had never existed before and he saw it as a footpath that led into a world that was sensual and manyfaceted and complex beyond his understanding, but for the moment he was comfortable in it and roofs and shelter and ill weathers were things of no moment. He thought the only dwelling he needed was the unconfined and unwalled world itself.

MEMOIRS

Time Done Been Won't Be No More

THE MAN IN THE ATTIC

THAT YEAR THERE SEEMED NO place to keep warm. Wintertime in New York town, the wind blowing snow up and down the streets, sleet spinning against the glass storefronts, wind coming gritty and razorous out of the mouths of alleys, cutting through your clothing to the bone. This was the last of 1963, the cusp of '64: Kennedy was in the graveyard and Johnson in the White House, and something was in the wind. The first hints of disquiet in the air. Some dire chord had been strummed, the vibrations were rolling outward, wars and rumors of wars.

Drunk on the rhetoric of Thomas Wolfe, I had left my home in the South and come looking for experience. I had determined to open myself to everything the world had to offer, good and ill, to accumulate life and hoard it like a miser and, at some more contemplative point, try to make sense of it. I had joined the Navy, and now I was in Brooklyn, where Thomas Wolfe had walked the midnight streets and chanted, I wrote ten thousand words today. The Navy had promised travel and experience, and so far it was working out. I was new at the job, but already I had been hassled by cops and hustled by folks in the financial end of the love business, beaten up by Canadian Airmen in Esquimalt, by a street gang in Brooklyn and by a surly bartender in Long Beach. Experience was unfolding itself to me like a flower.

I even had a girl. Her name was Sara and she had almond eyes and long, straight chestnut hair. She was a freshman at a city college and she was into social causes like the burgeoning civil-rights movement. She loved poetry and books and music. She even believed me when I told her I was going to be a writer. We had met in the summer and been together as often as we could through the fall and winter. It was understood that we were soulmates, that we would always be together.

We hung out mostly in the Village, looking for the already ancient footprints of Ginsberg and Kerouac, listening for the fading chants of the Beat Poets, listening to jazz and folk music and blues in the cafés and coffee houses. I was in my civilian clothing, trying to blend, but already the world was aspiring toward a hip scruffiness the Navy wouldn't tolerate and I had to make do with my regulation haircut and polished shoes.

One night we were in a coffeehouse when a girl sang a song unlike anything I'd ever heard. This place was a basket-house, a club where musicians who didn't have paying gigs could perform a set then pass the basket around the audience. If you liked the songs you'd drop a half-dollar or handful of change.

This song seemed to be called, "Don't Think Twice, It's All Right" —that was the refrain that ended every chorus. It sounded full of contradictions--traditional in form yet new in sentiment, a love song and a kiss-off, hard and soft, tough and tender at the same time. It was a way of looking at things, a way of turning a hard exterior toward a world always looking for your weaknesses, and it came at you from all over the place. It was bathed in a gothic twilight, roosters crowing at the break of dawn, with more departures down long lonesome roads than a noir novel. It was love and bitterness swirled together: Goodbye's just too good a word, babe. So I'll just say fare-thee-well.

I have to talk to her, I told Sara. I want to know where she learned that song.

I don't think so, Sara said. You just want to meet that singer.

We met her anyway.

Haven't you heard of Bob Dylan? This is a Bob Dylan song. He's got a lot of others, too, and they're all great.

Bob Dylan. I had a vague memory of reading his name in a Nat Hentoff *Playboy* article on folksingers. But Hentoff hadn't mentioned this.

The next weekend Sara took me uptown to a record shop she said carried everything, and I bought two Bob Dylan albums. The second one, *The Freewheelin' Bob Dylan*, had "Don't Think Twice" on it. Listening on the phonograph in Sara's bedroom I realized the words were only half the story: the song was at least half attitude, acting, role-playing something. As if James Dean had merged with Rimbaud and Raymond Chandler and strapped on a flat-top Martin.

And I realized something else. You couldn't duplicate this, this was a one-time thing. Spend a lifetime learning the picking, and you couldn't get it the same way twice. Learn every shading and nuance of voice, and this would still be the only one in the world. Even Dylan couldn't duplicate it, try to Xerox it and the machine would short-circuit and smoke and burn. I felt there was no precedent for this that you could trace folk music back through its entire history, and you would not hear anything like this. The song and the song's performance came out of someplace raw and powerful, painful as an open wound. It was a way of looking at things in a single frozen moment of time.

Of course there were other songs on the album, and sure enough, they were all great. There was even a song that evoked Sara, a Girl from the North Country, where snowflakes fall and the wind hits heavy on the borderline, a girl with hair that hung long and rolled and flowed all down her breast. Of course, more properly this was the East, not the North, but to the heart, the points of the compass are not only useless, but irrelevant.

In the fullness of time, "Don't Think Twice" showed up on all the jukeboxes. Not by Dylan, but by Peter, Paul and Mary, who'd made it a moderate hit. Every bar and restaurant we went to, I rolled a lot of change down the throats of jukeboxes.

I didn't notice that Sara was becoming much vexed with the song until it was too late. I had suspected something was amiss. Long silences had crept into conversations that previously held no space for them. I would glance at her, and she would be watching me in a sort of speculative way. Perhaps our souls did not interlock as perfectly as we'd thought.

I'm sick of that damn song, she finally said. And I may have misjudged you. Your taste. He can't sing, and not only that, but he's not a poet, the way you say he is. It's ridiculous, that rooster crowing at the break of dawn crap. Does he assume everyone owns a rooster? I've never even seen a rooster. And he's always walking down those long lonesome roads. It's just sentimental bullshit.

I was outraged. Sentimental was the kiss of death, bullshit was even worse. Her own taste was now being called into question. It's not sentimental. Romantic, maybe, but not sentimental.

Romantic sentimental narcissistic bullshit. You only like it because it's the way you think. Or the way you'd like to think. And it's not only that. He's got into your head. You've gotten too far into this stuff, and you've let him into your head. It's warped your whole philosophy.

My philosophy? Well, this was a hell of a note. Here I didn't even know I had a philosophy, and the damned thing was warped. Broken before I even had a chance to use it. I tried to protest. This wasn't another girl. It wasn't another guy. It was a song, and I should be able to turn this thing around.

If you'd think about it, I said, you could change your mind and stay.

Her eyes went cold. She was receding already, accelerating through the red shift, a girl from the North Country seen through the wrong end of a telescope. I had inadvertently paraphrased a line from the song, and naturally she'd recognized it.

Stabbed in the heart. Here on the dark side of the road. The future yawned before me. Years of the Navy to go, I was barely out of the starting gate. Our lives together forfeit. Our house unbuilt, our children unconceived. Nothing to do, nothing to say. Except goodbye's too good a word, babe. So I'll just say fare-thee-well.

Orders had come through, my ship was leaving New York. It was cold the morning we got underway. Rain, mist off the sea like pale smoke. Sara's father came aboard to see me off. We stood awkwardly on the fantail, the sea choppy, the ship rocking against its lines. He was glad to see me go. He had never trusted my relationship with Sara, never trusted the breakup to last. He'd never trusted me. He asked prying questions, he watched me all the time, he stood with his ear pressed against Sara's bedroom door when we were in there, you could hear him there breathing.

He'll turn on you, he told Sara. They persecute Jewish people in the South.

I hadn't known that.

They even lynch them. They've done that in Georgia.

I hadn't known that either. I had never been to a lynching, never known anyone who had.

For some odd reason he'd brought his old duffel bag from World War II. He handed it to me with the solemnity of ceremony. I want you to have this, he said. I accepted it. It was heavy and I wondered what it was. Luger salvaged from the battlefield? The severed head of Hitler? Live hand grenades unpinned? A bomb with its clockwork whirring?

It was grapefruit. They were enormous. They looked like heavy pink bowling balls.

These are not your ordinary grapefruit, he said. These are expensive gourmet grapefruit. I hope that you can appreciate their quality. I hope you enjoy them. You can share them with your little friends.

I plan to, I said.

He took my hand again. He clasped it between both his own. The steel deck was throbbing through the floors of our shoes. His eyes were bulbous with the pleasure of containing so much joy.

Good luck on your journeys, he said.

And he went away, stumbling down the gangplank. My little friends were not terribly interested in grapefruit, gourmet or otherwise. They were inclined to toss them into the sea. Making a little game of it, trying to sink a floating grapefruit with a hurled grapefruit. For some reason I folded the duffle bag and stowed it under an arm. The duffel bag of the father of the girl from the North Country. The grapefruit began to drift back toward the shore, back toward Manhattan. Where I was not going.

The towers of New York reared above the cold choppy water. Manhattan was stamped against the horizon like a mirage, like a palace desire had conjured.

The grapefruit drifted toward the girl from the North Country as if homing devices were embedded in them. Look out your window, babe, and I'll be gone. Fare-thee-well.

Down through Cape Hatteras to the Panama Canal. Storms lay on the ocean. It seemed always night, always cold, everything felt wet with salt spray, everything tasted of sea salt. Seasick, homesick, heartsick for the girl from the North Country. Her image holographed in my memory, the taste of her mouth still on my tongue. Sick for the Village and espresso and the street freaks and poets, for Liam Clancy and Maria Muldaur and Mississippi John Hurt.

People had told me New York was cold and heartless. They had lied. I'd been invited into folks' homes and slept in their beds, ate at their tables. I'd had good times and interesting conversations. I had smelled Sara's hair, enjoyed soft flesh without the exchange of filthy lucre.

Now I was bound around the horn to San Diego. Where these things did not live. Where everything was sand and plastic palm jarheads who wanted nothing so much as to take you out into the alley and kick your sorry ass. Where merchants with cash-register eyes stood in the doorways of their jewelry stores and tailor shops and beckoned you to enter. Come in here, sailor. Easy weekly payments. Get an engagement ring for that girl back in the old hometown. A $20 watch for only a hundred bucks. Handmade suits of Italian silk that fit as if they'd been handstitched in the rain forest by spider monkeys.

And the men who cruised the bus stops like predators in late-model Volvos and Austin Healeys. In their sunglasses and golfing caps. Hey there, sailor, want a lift? How far are you going?

Nowhere near that far, good buddy.

And, oh my God, I'd just remembered. The drinking age in San Diego was 21, not New York's youth-accommodating 18.

The ship rolled and yawed. Folks strapped themselves into their bunks. I couldn't sleep. I lay and thought about what Sara had said, You've let him into your head.

Well, I'd concede that. But there was a precedent for it. Everyone has folks in their head. Already I had a few tenants up in those attic rooms. James Dean, Thomas Wolfe, William Faulkner. Flannery O'Connor had a lifetime lease, paid up forever. Faulkner had Melville and Conrad and Joyce. Even Dylan had Woody Guthrie and those beat poets and the French symbolists. And Little Richard. Woody had Joe Hill and Jesus Christ and maybe Abraham Lincoln. Lincoln had the founding fathers.

So what if I gave Dylan a room. He'd be the only musician. Always room for one more, just another towel in the bathroom, another place setting at the dining table. I could give him the room with that little gallery where

Carson McCullers used to sit in the twilight and watch the violet darkness seep into the soft Georgia landscape of her memory.

She'd be pissed and leave in a snit, but don't think twice, it's all right. She was outward-bound, anyway. She and Truman Capote had taken to scuffling and fighting and hissing like cats, and I was sick of the both of them.

Sometimes I could hear Dylan's boots on the stairs. He stayed in his room a lot, drinking, I think. He sat on his cot and tuned his Martin while McCullers, interrupted at her packing, screamed through the wall, You want to knock that shit off? It's three o'clock in the morning. Do you have to tune that thing at three o'clock in the morning?

Of course this attic was not a nice place to live. Sometimes, in fact, it was a sordid, squalid place. You couldn't have gotten Eudora Welty in there with a sawed-off shotgun. Walker Percy, slumming, sneered, waved a dismissive arm and hailed a cab for uptown. Its tenants drank too much and had indiscriminate and unprotected sex as often as they could, and when they weren't doing it they were thinking about it in a constant state of tumescence. Regret and loss tinged the windowpanes, darkened the fading wallpaper. Once, Faulkner passed out sitting with his back pressed against the hot radiator and when they kicked down the door and peeled off his polo shirt the vertical brown burn marks on his back looked like the bars on a window.

This place was set on the wrong side of the tracks and too near them. There was shouting and glass breaking at hours far past midnight. In the dark, freight trains went highballing past, their shrieks honing away to a thin remnant of loss that was like a taste on the back of your tongue that made you want to go with them and see the unknowable landscape they were arc-welding out of the night. The deferential ghosts of James Agee's Alabama sharecroppers hovered in the hallways or crouched figuring with their fingers in the dust on the floorboards, spectral and transparent revenants toting up the ciphers of lives that always came up wanting.

Dylan didn't seem to mind. He settled in. Sometimes I could hear him coughing. Sometimes his typewriter went on pecking until dawn.

On leave, preparatory to shipping out for the South China Sea, I imported Dylan to Lewis County, Tennessee, bought him in like contraband in my sea bag. Three albums now. Two friends and my brother and myself sat in my brother's room grouped around the stereo.

I didn't say that I had been listening to him for months and that I'd decided he was a visionary and part prophet, or that I was so far into the words I might never get out or even want out.

The needle hissed on the vinyl. The guitar picking seemed to come out of some old, lost, absolutely timeless place. It could've been a hundred years ago or next week. The voice, when it came, was always unexpected. You were hearing it for the first time no matter how many times you'd heard it before, the voice weary and resigned and pissed off all at the same time, it ain't no use to sit and wonder why, babe, iffen you don't know by now.

Son of a bitch sure can't sing, my friend said, his ears forever spoiled by mainstream Elvis and Johnny Mathis.

He can't blow that French harp either, the other friend said.

I didn't protest. I'd heard all this before. He's a good guitar picker, I said again.

But my brother, who was learning to play then and whose instrument was never more than an arm's reach away, picked his guitar up from the bed. He leaned and carefully set the tone arm back. When the guitar came again he started turning the keys and plucking strings, matching the tuning that was coming out of the speakers. When he was satisfied, his left hand began feeling around the strings, experimentally for the chords.

Calendar pages riffled, blew away in the wind, it was another year. I was in the Gulf of Tonkin in the South China Sea, war smoldering like a banked fire. Eight-inch guns hammered and hammered and paint flaked off the galley ceiling like harsh gray snowflakes. The ship maneuvered to avoid conjectural torpedoes. On the decks of our carrier, jets came and went and came and went, left loaded and returned empty in a seemingly endless cycle. On the beach, the fires from ammunition dumps flared and ebbed all night. By day, burning oil refineries smoked and stank.

Already I was looking forward to getting the hell gone. Something didn't quite compute here. What was happening never matched what I was reading about in the paper. There seemed some grotesque disparity between event and event's recounting.

Still, there was Dylan. Four albums now. On the new one, the songs were different, surreal images were becoming more and more common. These songs flickered around the edges. They were becoming more personal, their concerns moving from the ills of society toward some interior landscape. Less protest music. He seemed to have decided it was a lost cause. He confided in the hallway that he sometimes felt as if he were charged with holding together a world already faulted, leaking and determined to come apart at the seams. The folk-music business expected him to do this. He was tired of it. He didn't think he could do it. He didn't think the world was going to last.

I was keeping the music to myself. Dylan was an acquired taste nobody I knew was interested in acquiring. I had one of those small phonographs, the kind that closes like a suitcase, not unlike the one Anse Bundren's new wife is carrying at the end of *As I Lay Dying,* and I kept it with my records in the computer room that was my workspace. I would go there in the small hours of the night and write and listen to music.

I had a lot more records now: blues and folk and the new singer/songwriters who were working Dylan's side of the street.

Timing is everything. I was playing the album, *Another Side of Bob Dylan*, a song called "All I Really Want to Do." To the untrained ear this song is particularly grating. There's a part where his voice rises and rises and pulsates until it screeches into a sort of yodeling giggle. It's great, and funny as hell, but there are folks who regard this moment as a perpetual fingernail on an interminable chalkboard.

McPherson, my leading petty officer and boss, chose this moment to come through the hatch and see what was going on. If it had been another song, a moment earlier or a moment later, everything might've gone down differently.

He gave a sort of strangled inarticulate cry. He seemed taken with some manner of fit. His mouth was a horrified O, his eyes bulged in agony. He clasped his hands to his ears. God almighty damn! He screamed, and ran across the deck and jerked the cord from the wall. He grabbed up my records blindly   Dylan, Joan Baez, Brownie McGhee, Jimmy Reed.   He jammed them between the lid and turntable and forced the lid down and grabbed up everything and whirled and went through the hatch. I could hear him going up the ladder to the main deck.

I followed him. He was at the rail. The deck rose and fell in the chop.

Drown this caterwauling son of a bitch, he said.

He hurled everything into the sea, albums skipping like Frisbees, the phonograph listing and filling with water, going down for the third time, do not resuscitate.

He turned and went without a word.

I stood watching the records drift toward the shore. Like messages sent into space, hello out there. I wondered what the Vietcong would make of these strange cultural artifacts. All these drowned bluesmen and Cambridge girls with ironed-looking hair. I imagined them putting Dylan on the turntable, lowering the tonearm. Scratching their heads in perplexity. Goodbye's just too good a word, babe. So I'll just say fare-thee-well.

Timing is everything. When I stepped off the plane that had flown me from Japan to Long Beach for discharge, a crewman's tinny radio was blasting away. I stepped into the hot glare of sunlight, and a familiar voice was demanding, How does it feel? To be on your own? A complete unknown? With no direction home? Like a rolling stone?

That sounds like Dylan, I thought. But the music sure doesn't. What the hell's happened here? Dylan hadn't been in his room for a few months. He was on the road, more changes in the wind.

There was more strangeness around. Changes abounded, they seemed to be the order of the day. I'd been gone eighteen months. In days to come I saw men on the streets with hair down to their shoulders, people carrying signs protesting the war. Something's happening here, but you don't know what it is, do you, Mr. Jones? I saw rock music on primetime TV, a show called *Hullabaloo*. The Byrds were singing Dylan, granny glasses, more long hair. McGuinn was even phrasing like Dylan. I saw a duo calling themselves Sonny and Cher. They looked like Brill Building hippies. They were singing a song called "I Got You Babe". The words were drivel except for one word. Babe? Where's that Babe coming from? They're stealing from Dylan, picking his pocket, ripping him off like a Tijuana pimp. Where's a cop when you need one?

More calendar pages blowing in the wind, a veritable snowstorm of them. Time passes slowly up here in the mountains, the world goes its weary way. Dylan and I grow older. He's much on the road these years, identities flicker like frames in a film. He's a family man, a gypsy rover, a whiteface minstrel, a born-again Christian. He's an 80-year-old bluesman from the Mississippi Delta: masks shuffle like cars in a deck. I try a few masks of my own.

Then comes a day when the attic is almost deserted. Except for Dylan, the tenants are long gone. Who knows where, perhaps they're winos living like street people. Heroes have feet of clay, they stand on shifting sands. A man must make his own way. A cold wind blows down Desolation Row, the ambulances are long gone, the sweeping Cinderella is so far past the age of being easy, her Bette Davis style is a grotesque vamping.

A man could learn to live listening to Woody Guthrie, Dylan said a long time ago. I believe that this is just as true of Dylan. You could learn to live listening your way through all those albums. Especially if you have an affinity for masks and one-eyed jacks and shifting identities: now you see me, now you don't.

And you learn to accept growing older. You become aware of mortality. The sun lowers, hovers over the horizon. I got new eyes, Dylan marvels. Everything looks so far away.

Don't think twice, it's all right. The more things change the more they stay the same.

A man must make his own way, and you grow too old for heroes. But Dylan and I go back a long way, we've been through a lot together, and you never grow too old for a friend, even one you've never met.

Presidents come and go, and empires rise and crumble, but Dylan's still on the road. The never-ending tour rolls on to its inevitable end. But nobody's giving up here, nobody's getting old. On *Love and Theft*, the most recent studio album, Dylan sounds positively rejuvenated, shot full of some kind of goat-gland tonic, funny as Charlie Chaplin, brash as Robert Johnson and wise and fatalistic as Mississippi John Hurt.

So jump into that hopped-up Mustang Ford, babe, and throw your panties overboard. This ride's not over yet.

And hey girl from the North Country: Goodbye's just too good a word, babe. So I'll just say fare-thee-well.

CALVES HOWLING AT THE MOON
–To accept art you have to accept mystery–

I'M NOT AN ARTIST, I just paint for the reasons most people do the things they like, because they're fun and because of the satisfaction you get when you have completed (or decided you've completed) a picture. And because you have an idea in your head, you try to paint pictures that equal it. They never do, but the feeling that you get a little closer each time is part of that satisfaction.

The first painting that ever affected me deeply was by Andrew Wyeth. I was in elementary school, about the fourth grade. Wednesday was library day, and although most of the books were off-limits to fourth graders, I looked forward all week to roaming around the shelves, and picking out titles that I promised myself I would read one day.

The librarian controlled us with an acerbic tongue and a fierce eye, but she liked me for a couple of reasons: because I could refold a newspaper and keep all the sections in order (If he can do that, I don't know why the rest of you can't) and because I had once asked her how much she had to pay to be in charge of all those library books.

She noticed that I was always drawing pictures, comic-book panels with Zane Grey Westerners

- 119 -

pummeling each other with their fists or battling with six-guns.

She was also the high-school librarian, and one day she brought down from there a coffee-table book of prints of great American paintings. She told me I could take it home and study it for a few days. Look at something besides trash, she said. But don't tear it. And don't spill anything on it.

The picture that grabbed me was *Christina's World*. Wyeth had painted a woman crouching on a grassy slope, who awkwardly faces away from the viewer, toward a New England farmhouse. Years later I read that the woman was disabled and that Wyeth had painted her climbing the hill in the only means of locomotion available to her. But the knowledge was not necessary to appreciate the painting. What affected me about the painting was its mystery. The background story neither deepened the mystery nor explained it. It was like that Frost poem about stopping by the snowy woods, miles to go before you sleep. The woman seemed affected by the gravity or enormity of something just out of view. To me, as a child, *Christina's World* needed an explanatory panel before and following it.

If you're doing a job for someone, say building a chicken coop, you have to build it the way you were hired to build it. Plumb and square, the size just so. A story or a song or a painting is your own chicken coop and you can build it the way you damn well please.

The first picture I made that I actually thought of as a painting was a present for my father. I was in the Navy then, the Vietnam War was going full-tilt, and I was on a destroyer in the South China Sea. Privacy was hard to come by, and late at night, when everyone except the watch section was asleep, I used to ease down to my work station, the computer room, to read and write. I decided to paint there.

My father had this thing about images of wolves and trains. I guess they represented a yearning for a world free from timeclocks and Sears payments and folks waiting for the food to be set out on the table. Now Christmas was approaching and I was going to paint them: three wolves on a snowy slope, a gauzy yellow moon to bay at, their breath smoking in the icy air.

I was well into it at three o'clock in the morning when the hatch sprang open and my division officer burst through it with a calculator in hand. The ship was rife with rumors that China was coming into the war to aid the North Vietnamese, and the officers spent a lot of time figuring the distance from mainland China and how long it would take jet fighters to reach the fleet. He was inside the room abrupt and sudden, his eyes sweeping for an uncapped bottle, his nose sniffing for marijuana, his ears straining to pick out the diminishing footsteps of naked Taiwanese prostitutes.

What the hell are you doing down here?

Trying to paint, I said.

He looked at the consoles, the walls.

Oh, he said, a picture? You're painting a picture? You're not even supposed to be here. You're supposed to be in your rack, not wandering around the ship all night. We're at war here, not running some art school. That's mighty suspicious behavior.

I was just working on a Christmas present for my father, I said.

He came over to look. He squinted one eye, like a jeweler with his loupe screwed in. He shook his head, They look a little fluffy to me, he said.

A little what?

Fluffy. Plump. Chunky. Hell, look at the shoulders on those suckers. They look like young cows. You've painted calves there, howling at the moon.

Well, so be it. Perhaps they were wolves who'd bulked themselves up on steroids and were grouped there baying at the moon, patiently awaiting the judgment of a congressional committee. Or perhaps they were not wolves at all, but offspring of dark and dangerous liaisons between seemingly incompatible beasts who had some black and lonely night been of a fey and experimental frame of mind.

Well, they were my wolves, or whatever the hell they were, and they looked like whatever I had painted onto the canvas. Maybe art is striving for the perfect wolf. The world is wide, you can walk toward the horizon the rest of your life and never reach it.

This was a long time ago, and the military is probably different now. Perhaps one is issued palette and brushes upon induction. But I decided it was unwise to paint aboard ship in the small hours of the morning. One's motives, one's very gender, seemed called into question. If, during a war, the compulsion to paint is overwhelming, Warhol-like silkscreens of AK-47's might be acceptable. Jack Dempsey slamming the canvas. Best to avoid still lifes of light caught in wine bottles and artfully arranged pears. Perhaps best to avoid fruits altogether.

Just as if you are a closet writer by night, and work in a construction crew by day, you do not come on the job site interrupting conversations about football and deer hunting, with tales about the fragility of typewriter ribbons. This is just the way things are, it is the way of the world. If you have a secret identity to protect, if you are wearing a costume under your work clothes, you do not cross a landscape strewn with Budweiser cans and 30-06 casings trailing sheets of foolscap and calling out, *Goddamn, boys, listen to this sonnet I wrote over the weekend.*

The southern part of the county I live in is abandoned. It used to be owned by a mining company. The people who lived here, sometimes thirty families to a single hollow, are long dead, their children long dead. As the ore played out, the people played out with it. Nothing left but the graveyard, the stones weathernworn and tilted, the graves violated by tree roots and the burrowing of animals. Nothing left but broken glass and fallen brick and drilled holes forty feet deep.

It is a good place to find subjects to paint or to write about because it is a place obsessed with time, by the lives once lived here, the very atmosphere scored by hard times and rough ways. Listen closely and you can hear the timbre (but not the words) of long-gone conversations. All these lost lives seem to exist and to go on uninterrupted around you and every life exists simultaneously, every one layered like stacks of imaged glass that, held to the light, show all these past lives without precedence or priority, time itself having become pliable and of no moment. If you try to paint this landscape, a force that is invisible and just outside the frame (but there all the same) seems to affect whatever you are laying on the canvas.

I have a friend in Alabama who makes wind chimes from found objects. Though he has published a novel Hollywood made into a movie, he is known locally as The Wind Chime Man. His front yard tends down toward Mobile Bay and is thick with live oaks from whose branches hang Spanish moss and his creations, which are like bizarre fruit, graceful or absurd or eerily beautiful. As the wind whistles through them, they clash gently like frozen leaves.

He finds suitable props on roadsides and at garbage dumps and he keeps objects he hasn't yet found a place for in boxes: ancient bluegreen bottles that have imprisoned rays of light so that they gleam even in darkness, lost or discarded costume jewelry, the replevied engines of Lionel model trains.

I sat on a lawn chair one day and watched him work. He'd try an object, back off, and see if it matched whatever picture he had in his head, and try another one.

You've got enough of those things for all the front porches in the world, I said. Why do you keep making them?

He looked impatient, irritated. He shook his head. It's therapy, he said. It keeps my mind occupied. Keeps me out of trouble. Besides, people won't let me alone. They drive here from as far away as Atlanta and pay me three or four hundred dollars apiece for these things. They got to have some selection to pick from.

But he thought about it while he worked, because he knew I really wanted to know.

I just want to make something I'd like to look at, he said. Something that looks right.

All right. That works for me. Maybe art is just coming up with something you'd like to look at, whether it springs from dream or vision or nightmare.

I know another sculptor who was hired to build an animatronic horse for a Hollywood action movie. It had to be absolutely lifelike so that it could stumble and die broken-necked onscreen and no one save the ASPCA would be the wiser. It took a long time, but what he built required da Vinci's knowledge of anatomy, the wise hands of Michelangelo, patience that would have taxed Job.

Is that art or commerce? I don't know, but he also welds scrap metal into strange animals that few people pay him for. He joins discarded automobile axles and children's tricycles and broken lawn chairs into constructs that look like creatures that have staggered from the tangled undergrowth of the imagination into reality, shaking their heads and blinking their eyes against the brightness, aghast at this world they've been brought into against their will.   He also creates Goldbergian machines that look as though, given the proper voltage, they could power the world or short-circuit it.

Sometimes he sells one, but that's not the point, that's not the reason he does it.   He doesn't ponder much on why he does it.   Perhaps they're just something he'd like to look at, and maybe the world needs artists to dream while the world sleeps, to go into the unknown where on ancient maps the old cartographers drew dragons. (Sometimes they old cartographers were right.)

Artists are like the astronomers who postulate the existence of unknown planets by the pull of their gravity on known celestial bodies.   The mystery is invisible but felt, just outside the frame, tugging gently at whatever is within it, unknowable until the next panel is painted.

PAINTINGS

William Gay

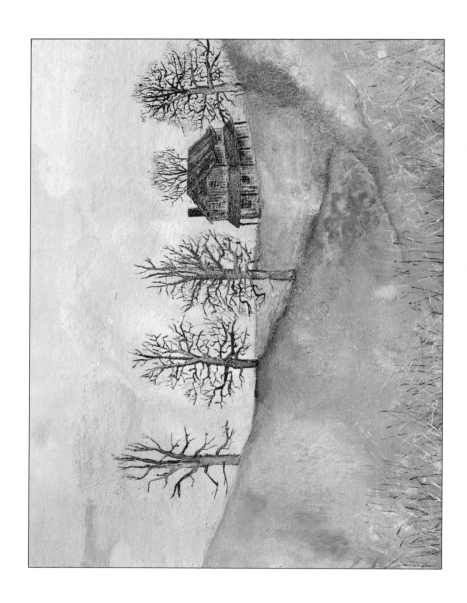

QUEEN OF THE HAUNTED DELL
–An authenticated history of the night the bell witch followed us home–

HERE'S WHAT HAPPENED OR MAYBE HAPPENED OR IS SUPPOSED TO HAVE HAPPENED:

Adams, Tennessee, is in Robertson County, five miles from the Kentucky line. In 1804, when John Bell moved his wife and six children and slaves to a thousand-acre farm he'd bought on the Red River, Adams was a virtual wilderness. Skirmishes with Indian war parties up from the south were less than twenty years in the past. The Indians didn't live here, but it was sacred ground to them and had been for thousands of years since the time of the Mound Builders. It was also theirs by right of treaty. As was often the case, the treaty had clauses and fine print and footnotes, and the land was soon settled by prosperous white landholders, most of them from North Carolina.

John Bell was prosperous, too, but he seems to have had a clouded past. There were rumors of his being involved in the death of his former overseer. By all accounts he was a close man in a business deal as well, and it wasn't long before he found himself in Robertson County civil court accused of usury in a slave trade with a woman named Kate Batts.

These things about Bell, by the way, are not folklore or hearsay. They're a matter of public record, but they are not mentioned in the early books about the Bell Witch, which paint John Bell as a sort of stoic martyr.

Because of his legal trouble, Bell was excommunicated from the Baptist Church, and in a small community where almost every social function is tied in one way or another to the church, this was a big deal. Living in such a close-knit community of God-fearing folk, Bell must have felt like a pariah.

Then things got worse.

In 1817 John Bell saw an animal in his cornfield. It looked like a black dog but not exactly. When he fired his rifle, it vanished. Not long after, Betsy, Bell's thirteen-year-old daughter, was picking flowers and saw a girl dressed in green swinging by her arms from the branches of a tree. The girl in green vanished.

There were noises in the house. Something gnawing on the bedposts, rats maybe, the sound of something enormous and winged flying against the attic ceiling, the sound of chained dogs fighting. Lights flitted about the yard. Covers were yanked from folks trying to sleep. Hair was pulled, jaws slapped. Betsy seemed to catch the worst of it.

This went on almost every night for a year before Bell confided in anyone outside the family. According to M.V. Ingram's *An Authenticated History of the Bell Witch*, published in 1894 and based on an account written by one of Bell's sons, things had come to such a sorry pass, nerves were frayed, nobody was sleeping, that Bell had to have help and opinions. Two preachers were consulted, James Johnson and Sugg Fort.

Bell was a stern and autocratic man who had been able to keep the news of the disturbances confined within his family. But as soon as he confided in others, the cat, or whatever the hell manner of beast it was, was out of the bag and gone.

The self-styled investigators soon determined that there was an intelligence behind the phenomenon. It would respond to knocks and answer questions: one knock for yes, two knocks for no.

Odd as this may be, it did not set a precedent. A similar case had taken place in Maine in 1800. It happened again in Surrency, Georgia, and again in 1848 in Hydesville, New York, to a family named Fox. The Foxes were more amenable to this sort of thing, and within months they were holding séances and playing the ectoplasm circuit, giving birth to the great Spiritualist movement of the nineteenth century.

The witch, they had begun to call it this almost by default, no noun seemed adequate, thrived under all the attention she was getting. At night the yard would be full of wagons and buggies, the house full of folks putting the manifestations to the test. Apparently Bell turned no one away: he was hoping somebody could figure out all of this and put it to rest. So word spread, and the witch became a source of entertainment. Recreation was in short supply in Robertson County in 1817, and this was better than a pie supper, a church social, a cornhusking, as long as you could go home when the show was over and leave it where it was.

The Bell family couldn't do this. The witch seemed to have moved in to stay. Then she developed a voice. First a sibilant whisper, than a strangled sort of gurgle. Eventually she began to sing gospel songs and to speak. From contemporary accounts (and there are a lot of them), the voice was very odd-sounding: Metallic and somehow mechanical, it did not sound much like a human voice at all. From today's perspective it seems the witnesses were trying to describe a computer-generated voice, perhaps like the one in your telephone that asks you to punch a number for more information.

And information was what they wanted. *What are you? Where do you come from? What do you want?* they asked her.

There was no shortage of answers. In fact, she appeared a little perplexed herself. Pressed for the truth, she seemed not to know what she was, and as parapsychologists have discovered, if spirits exist, they're terrible liars.

I am a spirit that has always been and will always be, she told them. *I am everywhere and nowhere.* Or she was the spirit of an Indian whose bones they'd disturbed. Or she was the spirit of a man who had buried an enormous amount of money on the Bell farm and wanted them to find it. Finally she said: *I am no more or less than Kate Batt's witch, and I am here to torture and kill old John Bell.*

The Bell family came to refer to this four-year period as Our Family Trouble, and during that time there was a seemingly endless stream of folks arriving and departing. A few years before he became president, Andrew Jackson even considered it an adventure worthy of his reputation. He came with an entourage and wagons and tents and provisions, planning to stay a couple of weeks. But the spirit took offense to a professed witch killer they had brought along and ended up pulling his hair and humiliating him with slaps.

After two days the group unceremoniously packed up and left.

Many came intent on proving that the whole thing was a hoax. People had noticed that Betsy went into a trance before the entertainment commenced. The family thought of these as fainting spells, and it was only *after* Betsy came out of these trances that the spirit would speak. Some folks felt that she was drawing some sort of energy from her. Others decided that Betsy was a ventriloquist and that the whole thing was an elaborate put-on. But according to a contemporary account, a man once grasped Betsy and held a palm tightly across her mouth, and the voice went on unchanged and undeterred.

The entertainment apparently varied from the gospel to the x-rated and all points in between. The witch was a malicious gossip, and she delighted in relating the sexual doings of the crowd. Betsy was by now engaged to Joshua Gardner, and she was fond of taunting Betsy with knowledge of indelicate matters that should have been private. The witch had a scatological sense of humor, and the house was often filled with the odors of vomit and excrement. If one can suspend disbelief long enough to picture it, the scene must have been like a rustic talk show, reality TV and an Early American motif and a disembodied host dealing in dirty linen and guilty secrets.

The witch had two stated purposes: to kill John Bell and to break up Betsy's impending marriage to Joshua Gardner. Bell died in 1820, a year before the cessation of the haunting. There is controversy about what he died from, but, predictably, the witch took credit, claiming that she had poisoned him. At his death, she filled the house with celebratory laughter and bawdy songs. According to Ingram's 1894 book, she sang *Row Me up Some Brandy-o* at Bell's funeral.

Her energies seemed much dissipated by Bell's demise. Though a shadow of her formerly robust self, she still had the strength to prevent Betsy's marriage. To quote from the diary *Our Family Trouble* by John Bell's son Richard.

Yet this vile, heinous, unknown devil, torturer of human flesh, that preyed upon the fears of people like a ravenous vulture, spared her not, but chose her as a shining mark for an exhibition of its wicked stratagem and devilish tortures. And never did it cease to practice upon her fears, insult her modesty, stick pins in her body, pinching and bruising her flesh, slapping her cheeks, disheveling and tangling her hair, tormenting her in many ways until she surrendered that most cherished hope which animates every young heart.

The witch left in 1821, saying that she would return in seven years. According to John Bell Jr., she did reappear but only to him and only briefly. No one was interested in her anymore. She was yesterday's news, and the Bell family was weary beyond measure of the whole affair. Slighted, the voice promised (or threatened, perhaps) to return in 107 years.

By now the Bell children had largely dispersed into homes of their own on the original property. Betsy married her former schoolteacher and remained in Adams. Her mother, Lucy, stayed behind to live, by herself, in the old farmhouse. John Jr. lived in his own home across from her.

The rest is a matter of legal documents: marriages, probated wills, death certificates. After Betsy's husband died in 1848, she moved to Panola County, Mississippi. Lucy died in 1837, and the old log house was subsequently dismantled. No one would have it, and none of the Bells wanted to move back and live there.

But the story was too outrageous to die. In the 1850s the *Saturday Evening Post* ran a story on the Bell Witch, postulating that Betsy was a ventriloquist and had faked the whole thing. Betsy sued for libel and won, settling for an undisclosed amount of money. Most of the family, as well as young Gardner, had scattered out of Adams County. It was as if everyone wanted some distance between himself and the growing legend.

In 1894 M.V. Ingram, after years of unsuccessful attempts, acquired the diary of Richard Bell and incorporated it into his *Authenticated History*. This account of the haunting was anathema to the remaining Bells as well as to their offspring, who considered the Family Trouble a shameful episode and their personal business. They were angry all over again in 1934 when Charles Bailey Bell published his own book, which included a recounting of his conversations with his great-aunt Betsy.

There are tales about bad luck following the Bells, about a family curse, but the history of any family is a history of death and misfortune.

So what, if anything but the birth of a folktale, happened?

Everyone who went looking for a solution found one, so there are ultimately more answers than questions and more culprits than victims.

1) It was a hoax perpetrated by Betsy Bell for reasons unknown, possibly a prank. She acquired the art of ventriloquism and put it to use.

2) It was a hoax perpetrated by one Richard Powell, who wanted to get rid of Joshua Gardner and John Bell and marry into the well-to-do Bell family.

3) It's true as told, and in the world as we know it there is no explanation.

4) Something happened, a poltergeist perhaps, but it's been grossly distorted by time and retelling.

5) It was black magic. Kate Batts was a witch, and this was her revenge on Bell.

6) Something happened. It's tied to a secret concerning Betsy Bell and her father, and the whole haunting is rooted in abnormal psychology.

7) The Bell farm is located on an ancient source of power, sacred to the Indians and whatever race came before them. Spirits have always been there, and they sometimes draw on energy wherever they can find it. According to theories about poltergeists, an unhappy household filled with adolescents would provide an almost inexhaustible supply of energy. (It might be worth pointing out that the spirit's powers waned as Betsy passed from adolescence to womanhood.)

There are other explanations, but this seems sufficient.

The first possibility seems least likely if any weight can be attached to newspaper accounts and sworn testimony. Hundreds of people apparently witnessed her. They all can't be lying. As for the second, it's hard to imagine how he did it, even if only a fraction of the accounts are true. Also, motivation seems questionable, and if you can sustain a practical joke for four years, naïveté must have run deep in Robertson County.

The last two reasons are more interesting. Nandor Fodor was a psychiatrist who investigated and wrote about poltergeists. In the 1930s and 40s he postulated that Betsy was sexually assaulted by her father when she was a child. She repressed the memory, but this repression erupted at the onset of puberty in violence against her father. Fodor points out that the witch came down hardest on Betsy and the elder Bell, implying at once that Betsy had feelings of revenge and guilt: Bell had to die, and to punish herself Betsy had to give up the man, Joshua Gardner, she loved.

But this theory isn't based on much, and Freudian psychology isn't the gospel it once was. It's about as easy to believe in malevolent spirits as it is disrupted psyches slamming things around and poisoning folks. It also seems to me a little tacky to accuse even a dead man of child molestation if you don't have the goods to back it up.

Colin Wilson is a British philosopher and an investigator of the paranormal. Poltergeists are pretty much his specialty, and he started out believing the conventional theory about adolescent energy. But he came to think that teenage energy running amuck didn't cover everything. He theorized that spirits that haunt places of power can utilize the frustrated energy of adolescents. Excess energy, violence, and unhappiness seem to provide a breeding ground for poltergeists and, Wilson says, spirits can come upon this energy and use it the way a child might kick around a football that he finds lying in a vacant lot.

In the end it seems you can twist the story to any frame of reference, hold it to the light, and turn it until it reflects whatever you want to see.

After the destruction of the Bell home, folks came to believe that the witch had taken up residence in a nearby cave, now called the Bell Witch Cave. The path to it is well-traveled. It has been worn down by writers, reporters, television crews, parapsychologists, skeptics, true believers, and throngs of the merely curious. The path winds steeply down the face of an almost vertical bluff.

The present owner of this section of the old Bell farm is Chris Kirby, and she's carrying a heavy-duty flashlight and leading the way. Underfoot is crushed stone, and the earth is terraced with landscape timbers to prevent the trail from eroding into the Red River, which is flowing far beneath us.

Past the guard rail you can see the river where the Bell sons used to flatboat produce down to the Cumberland and on to Mississippi and New Orleans. You can see the bench-like area of rock and brush that lies between the riverbank and the point where the bluff rises sheerly out of the bottomland. This is perhaps the only part of the Bell geography that remains virtually unchanged since 1817.

Betsy Bell, dubbed Queen of the Haunted Dell when she became the focus of the mystery, used to come here with Joshua Gardner and other young people on lazy

Sunday afternoons after the services at Red River Baptist Church. They'd fish in the river and picnic by the waterfall in the shade of the same huge oaks and beeches that are here now. At some point the young folks would separate into couples and go their own ways. Looking into the trees you can almost see them, your imagination can transform the sound of the waterfall into soft laughter.

At the mouth of the cave Chris turns toward us. People sometimes have problems photographing the entrance to the cave, she says. Sometimes there's a mist that blocks the front of it, or maybe things that look like faces or orbs of light turn up in the pictures. Things that weren't there. Sometimes cameras just fail.

Thirty feet or so into the cave there's a heavy steel gate.

People kept breaking in, and it's dangerous further back, Chris says, fitting a key into the padlock. That's why you had to sign a waiver. Kids keep trying to slip in here with their girlfriends to scare them.

If fear is an aphrodisiac and if a tenth of the things told about the cave are true, then this is the ultimate horror movie.

Inside the cave the first thing you notice is the temperature. It's a constant fifty-six degrees, and the Bell family, among others used to store perishables here. The second thing you notice is how impressively cave-like it is. This is no two-bit roadside attraction, no world's largest ball of twine, but a real cave, three stories laid one atop the other like a primitive high-rise, connected by crawl holes that wind upward through the first-floor ceiling.

A kid got stuck in one back in the 1800s, Chris says, shining the light into a jagged ascending tunnel. He was really stuck, he couldn't get out, and all at once a voice said, *Here, I'll get you out*, and the witch jerked him out. He was scared to tell his folks about it, but that night the witch told his mama, *You better put a harness on that boy so you can keep up with him*. Chris is fascinated by the Bell Witch story, and it's a fascination that predates her ownership of this cave. She's read all the books, and she says she's heard and seen a couple of things herself.

In the first large chamber there's a crypt perhaps a foot and a half wide by four and a half feet long, a child's crypt, chiseled out of rock. Large, flat rocks were shaped to fit vertically around the edges, and the body of a young Indian girl had been laid inside. More flat rocks for a lid, the hole covered over with a cairn of stone until a few years ago, when the cave's previous owner accidentally found it. The archaeologist who examined the bones said they were between two and three hundred years old.

If you can imagine someone laboriously chipping away at the rock and placing in the body, then it's not hard to see how private and personal this was, and suddenly it doesn't seem to be the sort of thing you should be paying five dollars to see.

In the next chamber Chris shows us where she saw a strange haze shifting in one corner. Farther back, five hundred feet or so into the bluff, the cave narrows until it's inaccessible. She shines the light. It's almost absorbed into the wet dark walls as the tunnel veers crookedly out of sight. You'd have to be a spelunker to crawl back in there.

That's where I heard the scream coming from, Chris says. Not any kind of animal, but a woman screaming. That's what that *Tennessean* camera crew heard, too.

We fall silent and listen, but all you can hear is the gurgling of underground water. If you listen intently enough, it becomes voices, a man and a woman in conversation, a cyclic rising and falling in which you can hear timbre and cadence but not the words, and in the end it's just moving water.

Outside in the hot sunlight you're jerked into another century. Inside it was easy to feel that all these events were layered together and happening simultaneously: the haunting, a wall smoked black by Native American fires, the crypt of bones, the laughter of young lovers exploring the cave. Outside it's just Adams, Tennessee, circa 2000, and a vague nostalgia for a place and time you've never been and can never go.

Chris is locking up the cave. Some people might talk to you, she says. But a lot of people won't talk about it at all. After that *Blair Witch* movie came out, this place was sort of overrun with reporters and writers. But some people around here don't think it's anything to joke about. Some of them have seen things and heard things and feel the whole business should just be left alone.

I don't really know what to think, Tim Henson tells me. I know something happened, but I've never really seen anything myself. I've talked to a lot of people who say they have. A friend of mine was fishing down in front of the cave and swears he saw a figure, a human figure, that just disappeared. And people say they see lights around that property. But I'm particular about finding an explanation for things I see and hear. And so far I've always been able to find an explanation that satisfies me.

Henson's the superintendent of the water department in Adams, but he's also the town's unofficial historian, a walking encyclopedia on the Bell family and their troubles, who can quote courthouse records and church rolls from the nineteenth century without having to look them up. He's the man that people come looking for when they're doing a book or a documentary about the Bell Witch. Most recently, he spent some time being interviewed for The Learning Channel. Henson comes across as a shrewd and intelligent man, and his take on the legend makes as much sense as any other I've heard.

It doesn't matter to me if it's true or not, he says. I guess *something* happened. There's about forty books now about it, and you don't write forty books about nothing. There's been three in the last year or so, and just the other day a fellow gave me a piece on the witch from an old 1968 *Playboy*. But I keep an open mind on all that. What I'm interested in is the story and the history, the Bells themselves and the way they interacted with their neighbors. There was a bunch of students down at Mississippi State University who tried to prove it was all a hoax, that Joshua Gardner hoaxed the whole county just to marry Betsy. But it's hard to say.

But folks still believe in it here? I asked.

Oh yes. Some do. And they figure it's not too smart to make fun of it or to get into it too deep. There was a couple here, a descendant of John Bell and one from Joshua Gardner. They fell in love and courted all their lives, but they were afraid to marry because of the Bell Witch.

When I was kid I read an issue of *Life* magazine about the seven greatest American ghost stories, and that was the first time I heard of the Bell Witch. Later my uncle, who was a great storyteller and had read the early books, fleshed out the tale. I found the books and read them myself, and for my money it's the quintessential ghost story. I figured that someday I'd go to Robertson County and see the Bell farm, which seemed to me an almost mythic place existing only in its own strange fairy-tale geography.

It was years before I made my first visit, more years still before I made my second.

The first I made with my uncle, whom I held in great esteem. I was beginning to read Steinbeck and Algren, and he seemed to be one of their characters come to life. He was sort of a restless-footed hard drinker, hard traveler, barroom brawler. Plus he had a tattoo on his bicep: a dagger with a drop of blood at its tip, a scroll wound round the blade that read, DEATH BEFORE DISHONOR. He had lied about his age to get into World War II, then crouched seasick and heartsick in the prow of a landing craft while the beaches at Normandy swam toward him like something out of a bad dream. He fought yard by yard across France and was wounded at the Battle of the Bulge. He was a hero, and he had the medals to prove it, though he didn't think they amounted to much.

After the war he bummed around the country, working where he could and riding freight trains, sleeping sometimes in places you don't normally want to associate with sleeping: jails, boxcars, graveyards. He was an honest and an honorable man, but he'd been down the road and back. He was what they used to call "a man with the bark on".

By the time we rode out to the Bell farm, a lot of time had passed, and he had settled down, quit drinking, and become a respectable family man.

At the time the cave was private property (it still is, but it's set up as a tourist attraction), and we weren't allowed to see it, let alone go inside. So we talked to a few locals, went looking for the graveyard and whatever remnants of Bell's old log home that might remain. The graveyard is in a cedar grove a mile or so off U.S. 41, and it's not easy to find. But it's been found time and again by vandals, who stole Bell's original tombstone and even dug up some of the graves. All that remains of the house are a few of the stones it used to stand on.

It was dark before we found our way out of the woods, and though we were trying to maintain a degree of detached curiosity, it was undeniable that this was an eerie place.

A few months later my uncle and his wife turned up at my house in the middle of the night with a strange tale. He looked nervous and haggard, far from the cool and collected man I was accustomed to. Something had jarred him, and he didn't take long getting around to it.

That thing has followed me home, he said.

Life had gone on, and I didn't know what he was talking about. What thing?

That Bell Witch, or whatever it is. We keep hearing things, seeing things. It's about to drive us crazy.

What kind of things? I asked.

We've heard voices. People mumbling, but you can't hear what they're saying. A hell of a racket that sounded like you'd dropped a chest of drawers from the ceiling and smashed it on the floor. You go look and there's nothing there. The other night I looked out the kitchen window and saw this ball of blue light just rise up from the ground and move off into the woods.

I didn't know what to say.

We want you to sleep in that bedroom where we hear that stuff, he said. If you hear something, at least we'll know we're not going crazy.

There was no way I wanted to do that. But by now I was trying to get down the road and back myself, and I had a reputation to maintain. I was also hoping this would turn out to be his idea of a practical joke.

All right, I said.

This is what I heard, or think I heard:

I couldn't sleep, and I kept a light on. At about three in the morning I was reading an old copy of

Reader's Digest when I heard a chuckle, a soft, malicious chuckle of just a few seconds' duration. It seemed to come from no particular point in the room.

I thought it was a joke. I jerked open the bedroom door. There was no one there. I went through the house. Everyone was asleep.

It was a long time until daylight.

What did I hear? I don't know. Did I really hear it at all? I don't know that, either, and I wouldn't argue it either way. It doesn't seem to matter. You hear what you believe you hear.

My uncle lives in West Tennessee near a town named after Joshua Gardner's brother, and I called him the other night.

Did you really hear all that stuff in that house, or were you just pulling my leg? I asked him.

We heard things right up until we sold the place and moved, he said. It sort of died down, but every now and then we'd hear something. You'll notice nobody lives too long in that house. It's changed hands several times since we sold it.

I told him I had been back to Robertson County and that I was writing an article about the Bell Witch.

It might be best to leave that stuff alone, he said.

I don't know if there's any truth in all this business. Because almost two hundred years have passed since the original haunting supposedly occurred, I don't suppose anyone else will know. But I do know that the world is a strange and wondrous place. There are mysteries on every side if you care to look. I also know that I don't know nearly as much now as I thought I did at twenty-five.   If I stacked the things I know next to the ones I don't, I wouldn't have a very tall stack

Every question is multiple choice, and truth depends on your frame of reference.   It sometimes seems an act of hubris to even form a conjecture.

I'd leave that stuff alone, I heard time after time from one source or another, and it might be worth remembering that the Bell Witch saved her strongest malice for scoffers and debunkers.   It might be wise to keep one's disbelief to oneself.

On the other hand, she was clairvoyant.   So it might be best not to think about that stuff at all.

MUSIC CRITICISM

Time Done Been Won't Be No More

TIME DONE BEEN WON'T BE NO MORE
(But See That My Grave Is Kept Clean)

SEE IT AS A TREASURE CHEST or, more aptly, a Pandora's box unleashing into the world not evil or hardships or death but ruminations and lamentations and commentaries upon them, fading picture postmarks mailed from a world that was already growing remote in 1952. That was the year Harry Smith released his *Anthology of American Folk Music,* and it must have been something to see: eighty-four songs on six LP records, two discs each for the three volumes, each volume with a title: *Ballads, Social Music*, and *Songs*. All in an elaborate, metal-hinged album accompanied by Smith's surreal liner notes in a homemade booklet festooned with occult and arcane symbols.

The LP format was new in 1952. No longer was a record restricted to one song per side. Now each side could contain a series of songs, and the producer could play with them, arrange them in any order he chose. This was a revolutionary concept, and Harry Smith made the most of it.

The *Anthology* is a case of the sum being greater than its parts, and Smith achieved this because he heard sounds not just as themselves, but in relationship to other sounds, and set out to make a sort of aural hologram.

Perfectly ordinary voices, even pleasant voices singing pleasant songs, are interred side by side with brief three-minute vignettes of darkness that light will not defray, horror that is only heightened by its contrast with the ordinary, so that some of the voices sound like screeches and mumbles and whispers leaked through mad-house walls, while the normal world continues without a misstep or altered heartbeat.

His thinking, in the sequencing of the *Anthology*, is so strange as to be almost beyond comprehension, but there's a clue on the cover of the original liner notes. A drawing shows the hand of God tuning a dulcimer to the Celestial Monochord, tuning it to a Heavenly harmony that unites Air, Fire, Water, and Earth. His plan was to tie together the four volumes of the *Anthology* in a similar fashion, but only three were released in 1952. (The fourth, which Smith apparently meant to represent Earth, was put out last year by Revenant Records.)

There wasn't much of a market for folk music in 1952, other than prettified versions of songs like "On Top of Old Smoky" and "Goodnight Irene," sweetened and made palatable enough for Your Hit Parade. To a generation of ears attuned to Perry Como and Patti Page, the *Anthology's* old hardscrabble songs full of loss and death must have sounded totally alien, rantings and ravings and exhortations from another dimension.

Although the bulk of the songs was recorded only twenty-five or so years earlier (between 1927 and 1932), they seemed to be coming out of a world far more remote than that. This was not easy-listening music, it was not soothing Muzak played in the background as you lived your life. This was darker stuff. There was something there, crouched down out of sight, but you had to squint to see it. You had to meet these songs halfway, and the halfway point was not always a pleasant place to be. Sometimes it was alien, too: a coal mine in West Virginia, a plank road that began nowhere and led circuitously back to the same place, a claustrophobic block in the French Quarter that existed nowhere save in the geography of Richard Rabbit Brown's "James Alley Blues", an old railroad camp (where Bob Dylan would find a verse he'd later use, like scrap lumber replevied to shore up "Stuck Inside of Mobile with the Memphis Blues Again"), an unreal geography in a cold, sourceless sepia light.

Stage props abound, jarring and dissimilar as symbols slid from the surface of a Dali painting: Kassie's watch, Dock Boggs's red rocking chair, the folding bed Furry Lewis's woman welcomed him to. It seems to be the setting for a thousand tales told long ago or tales not yet created.

Almost all this music came from the South, but it was a South folks figured themselves well shed of. There was something almost shameful about it. The South was trying to turn a face to the future, to catch up with the rest of the country in its pursuit of the American Dream. Post war prosperity had hit, rock n' roll was on the horizon, people wanted gleaming appliances in every kitchen and fish-finned cars in every garage. People wanted what was new, and this stuff was decidedly not new. It was primitive and unsophisticated, and folks would just as soon not hear it. It was the idiot child chained to the bedpost, the great-uncle who went to Texas and was hanged as a horse thief.

Which is all to say that the country was not waiting with bated breath for Harry Smith's *Anthology*. What is amazing is that enough copies fell into just the right hands. Hands that were maybe already tuning guitars or that would be compelled to pick up guitars by the sheer magnetism of the music these records contained– enough of the right hands to sow the seeds for the '60s folk revival and subsequent ones (or you could say that it never went away, just dropped off the Hit Parade). The present alt-country Americana movement and bands like Wilco still owe a debt to Harry Smith, which magazines like *No Depression* freely acknowledge. The whole Greenwich Village-Cambridge-San Francisco scene derived from it as did clubs like Gerde's Folk City, the Bitter End, the Troubadour and a panoply of performers as diverse as Dave Van Ronk, Phil Ochs, Joan Baez, Buffy Saint-Marie: the whole thing being chronicled in *Sing Out!* and *Broadside* magazines in a heady movement that in retrospect seems forever poised before the Kennedy assassination and Vietnam, a time when it seemed perfectly logical to believe that a song could change the world.

Van Ronk said, The *Anthology* was our Bible. We all knew every word of it, including the songs we hated. They say that in the nineteenth-century British Parliament, when a member would begin to quote a classical author in Latin, the entire house would rise in a body and finish the quote along with them. It was like that.

And then there was Dylan. It is not such a stretch to postulate that without Harry Smith, Dylan the folk singer would never have been. He certainly would have been different. Part of the legend he has propagated about his early years is that he once played piano in Bobby Vee's band. Vee was a minor teen idol around 1960, and there is an aching void between Bobby Vee and Harry Smith. So Dylan might only have been a variation on Bobby Vee or a white Little Richard, whom he used to emulate with his high school rock band.

It is unclear where Dylan first heard the *Anthology*. It is probably in the late 50s, when he was a student at the University of Minnesota and playing gigs at a folk club in Dinkytown, a raffish and bohemian district in Minneapolis. What is clear is that he heard it and took it to heart. (That's where the wealth of folk music was, he later said. It's all poetry, every single one of those songs.) His first album, released in 1962, contains his take on Blind Lemon Jefferson's "See That My Grave Is Kept Clean", from volume three of the *Anthology*, and one of his earliest songs, "Hard Times in New York Town", is a virtual rewrite of the Bently Boys' "Down on Penny's Farm", from the second volume.

Not that there's anything inherently wrong in this. From Robert Johnson to John Hurt to Furry Lewis, these old images and calls and responses roll down the years like echoes, like memories. Folk music and the blues have been constantly borrowed back and forth, reshuffled lines, put them in new surroundings, as if there is a vast supply of lines and metaphors and archetypes that serve as pieces that can always be assembled into new puzzles.

Popular culture critic Griel Marcus wrote an entire book to prove that the *Anthology* was the invisible substructure to *The Basement Tapes*, the fabled sessions that Dylan and The Band recorded in Woodstock in 1967, and the case he makes is more than persuasive.

But in the long haul none of this changes what Smith did, and from a perspective of time it seems scarcely to matter. None of this Dylan, The Band, John Cohen's New Lost City Ramblers, the folk movement, the fact that the *Anthology* resurrected the careers of musicians presumed long dead sums up Smith's accomplishment. In the end, the *Anthology* stands on its own as an eerie, prescient, and elusive piece of work, as if it had neither antecedent nor forebearer.

Sometimes the *Anthology* is a historical document. Sometimes it is a subjective comment on itself. Sometimes it's a mirror reflecting life back at you, casting a normal reflection, but then you move, and it's a warped fun-house glass that sends back the comic or grotesque or both. Occasionally it's even a scryer's crystal that lets you see further into the human condition than you wanted to see.

In an essay on the *Anthology* called Smith's Memory Theater, Robert Cantwell wrote, Listen to "I Wish I Was a Mole in the Ground" again and again. Learn to play the banjo, and sing it yourself over and over again, study every printed version, give up your career and maybe your family, and you will not fathom it.

Harry Smith was an American Original, as bizarre and one of a kind as the songs he struggled to preserve, and he seemed to veer back and forth between madness and a kind of incomprehensible genius.

The diverging path Smith followed all his life was staked out early. He was born in Oregon in 1923 to theosophical parents who dabbled in Freemasonry and the occult. His father once gave him an entire blacksmith shop as a birthday present, ordered Smith to learn alchemy and begin transmuting base metals into gold. Smith seems to have spent a number of years trying to accomplish this, but he was impoverished all his life so it's apparent he never did.

He said on several occasions that there was a strong possibility that he had been fathered by Aleister Crowley, an infamous black magic occultist who could, it was said, conjure demons and cast spells, but Smith was a mysterious man who was no stranger to masks and playing roles, and everything he ever said about himself had a quality of ambiguity to it.

Most of Smith's life was spent on the move, in pursuit of art. Smith's definition of art seems to be whatever he wanted it to be, and some of his obsessions were abstract to say the least: string figures, making hand-painted films that were by all accounts exquisite, recording sounds on tape (including the music of Native

American dances), ceremonial Easter eggs, paper airplanes--the list goes on.

Smith told a story about spending three days with Maybelle Carter, photographing a collection of patchwork quilts that she had, trying again to correlate color and sound, searching through Carter Family songs and quilts, trying to group the particular song with its matching quilt. One can only conjecture what Carter thought Smith was doing.

Smith was a sometime panhandler who was proud of his ability to live by his wits. He was a mesmerizing talker who managed to draw others into his visions, but he wasn't all talk. He was an intelligent man with a broad field of knowledge, some of it admittedly peculiar, and his mind seemed to make intuitive leaps, A to D without stopping at B and C, and he always knew what he was going on about even when he couldn't communicate it to others.

Smith lived always in a sort of impoverished Bohemia, first in the North Beach poets' area of San Francisco, then in Greenwich Village, then in the Chelsea Hotel in New York City. When the Beatnik movement arrived, it seemed to have been conceived exclusively with Smith in mind. For years he dwelt on its fringes. Allen Ginsberg put him up for a while, and Smith did the art for a volume of Ginsberg's poetry.

Essentially, though, he lived wherever he could get a roof over his head, preferably one large enough to cover the vast collection of *things* he was amassing. John Cohen interviewed him for a 1968 issue of *Sing Out!*

Here's what Cohen saw when he came through the door:

> The closet is filled with dresses
> from the Florida Seminole Indians. One
> corner of the room, marked with KEEP
> OUT signs, is filled with Ukrainian Easter
> eggs; on the bureau are stacks of mounted
> string figures; behind them is a movie
> camera alongside portfolios of his
> paintings and graphic work. In another
> corner is a clay model of a landscape
> which was recreated from a dream, piles
> of beautiful quilts and other weavings, as
> well as a collection of paper airplanes
> from the streets of New York. Small file
> cabinets of index cards are distributed
> between the pages of research books.
> Each book becomes more exotic by its
> juxtaposition with other such books,
> Mayan codices beside Eskimo
> anthropology studies under a collection of
> Peyote ceremonial paintings, etc., etc.

He once lost a huge part of his collection when he was evicted from a New York hotel, the landlord simply had it hauled away. But Smith had shifting interests, and he had grown adept at starting over.

All this time he had also been collecting phonograph records, anything that struck him as odd or different. These were mostly rural and what were then called race records. At one time he claimed to have owned a hundred thousand of them. He had always been obsessed with sound, but he said that his primary interest in recording was the technology of it. He was staggered by the idea that you could take what had always been an oral tradition and market it out of a Sears and Roebuck.

Always broke, Smith contracted with Moses Asch of Folkways Records to unload part of his collection. Then the deal was amended. A record assembled from his 78s would be issued, and Smith himself would compile it. It would turn out to be his major work of art.

As Cantwell wrote, Smith was creating a sort of memory theater, a mnemonic library, a primitive thinking machine that would, in Smith's words, program the mind.

The idea of a memory theater is one that fascinated Elizabethan England: an arena containing the entire cosmos of knowledge categorized by its cabalistic, astrological, and alchemical symbols, where scholars could enter at will and rummage through or pore over manuscripts. Smith never quite got away from alchemy.

In the beginning it sounds like most generic folk collections: Appalachian reworkings of English ballads, some reels and dance tunes, songs about house carpenters, errant wives, wagoner's lads. Performers like Uncle Eck Dunford, Buell Kazee. But entering Smith's world is like progressing down a carnival midway past the kiddie rides and Ferris wheels until you notice that the sideshows have grown stranger and stranger, that the barker's spiel has turned ambiguous, and that his features are stamped with sinister intent.

Deeper in the *Anthology*, things have changed. The songs are no longer child ballads or rustic reels or cautionary fables, and they are no longer distanced or detached but have become modal ballads that inextricably link singer and song. We have entered a realm where the words mean more than what they say because the performance is part of what is being said. The teller can no longer separate himself from the tale, they have merged to form something larger than both.

Some of the songs start out as if they were going to be straightforward renderings of actual events, then progress to ironic asides on these events, then to biographical tidbits about the singer himself. Furry Lewis's 1927 recording of Kassie Blues is one example. Originally released as Part One and Part Two and encompassing both sides of a 78 rpm record, it begins with an account of Kassie Jones, the fabled brave engineer. Then abruptly we're out of Jones's world and into Furry's, caught up in Furry's troubles with the law for bootlegging, with the woman who, when the police chase him to her door, bids him to her bed, then a jumpshot forward to Jones's children crying on a doorstep, comforted by a mother who assures them that the imminent pension is compensation enough for a father killed on the Southern Line.

In Part Two the guitar is more driving and urgent, and we're back with Jones, in his last minutes. The train's water is low, Jones's watch is slow, and he's bound for an appointment with a passenger train in a mythic non-future. All this tied together by a refrain that is sort of bluesman's ethos that has little to do with either a real or fictitious Casey/Kassie Jones. It's Furry, not Jones, who says of himself:

> I get it written on the back of my shirt
> I'm a natural-born easeman don't have to work.

In the third volume, titled simply *Songs*, we are in the dark heart of Smith's concept. At first the songs seem to have no connection with one another and are as disparate as the singers who sing them: Mississippi John Hurt, Rabbit Brown, the Carter Family, Dock Boggs. (Boggs's voice here sounds so dissociated it seems to be coming not just from some other time but from outside time itself, from beyond the pale, a voice half-filtered through a mouthful of graveyard dirt.) The music, especially the flailing banjos of Boggs and Macon, has a wild energy that is at once hedonistic and nihilistic so that the singer seems to be propelling himself headlong into oblivion, casting aside all the things you accumulate in life so that in the end there is nothing left but the energy itself. Kill yourself! Macon yells in "Way Down the Plank Road", and you don't know if he's talking to the audience or himself, but it scarcely seems to matter: Heaven's been abandoned, and Hell's too far away to worry about yet, and all that matters is rolling down the line.

The cumulative effect of the tracks reminds you of an old newspaper blown down an alley in the French

Quarter, revealing first one headline then another, documenting a world that is at best uncaring, at worst absolutely malevolent. Bad things happen within these pages, grainy black-and-white images flicker past and are gone. Children starve or freeze or are murdered, lovers betray and kill each other or remain faithful and die anyway, trains seem always to crash instead of reaching their destinations, assassinated presidents are in coffins taking their rest, the *Titanic* hits the iceberg (Wasn't it sad when that great ship went down? the singer asks sardonically). When farms fail in three successive songs, Smith seems to be making some gleeful point.

You marvel about the ability to laugh in death's face, to make jokes about starvation and joblessness and sadistic bosses and the chain gang, yet time and again you hear in these voices and words a dark stoicism. Perhaps only Uncle Dave Macon could have written a song about hard times and named it "Wreck of the Tennessee Gravy Train". Maybe that's a Southern trait, more likely it's a just human one.

The most dissonant note is struck by the song Smith chose to place next to last, Ken Maynard's rendering of "The Lone Star Trail", a stilted and clumsy pastoral that reminds you of the sound track to a bad 1940s Western, with Maynard singing nasally of rolling prairies and lowing cattle and smiling ranch foremen and the sweetest girl in the world. Placed anywhere else it could be an almost pleasant reverie, but taken in the context of what has gone before all those murders and dislocations and gone lovers and prison sentences, all underpinned with those sliding blues guitars, it's as out of place as a court jester at a funeral, and the ear is unprepared for such a sentimental vision of life. Perhaps Smith saw it as a joke, more likely he meant it to serve as a sort of pause, a screen saver, a time to consider the tale you have been told about a lost America, a kind of bookmark to set all this apart from the final song. This is Henry Thomas's "Fishing Blues", set to panpipes that sound older than America, older than anything. The sound is liberating, freewheeling, with an undercurrent of mystery not communicated by the words. On the surface it's just a song about getting a line and bait and a pole and going down to the fishing hole and catching a catfish, bringing it home, and frying it up. Baits and lines and poles normally have a sexual symbolism in blues, the fish is a sometime signifier for female sexuality. But there's nothing overt in the song, no innuendo in Thomas's voice, which makes the song stranger still. You notice not what is present but what is absent, Smith was well aware that the fish also represented spirituality, and it acquires this meaning only in the context that Smith has placed it in.

After repeated listenings you realize that Smith's genius was not only in selection but in placement, and that he had made a collage or crazy quilt of music in which everything matters, an impressionistic painting where every brushstroke counts.

In 1988 Smith became Shaman-in-Residence at the Naropa Institute in Boulder, Colorado, and longtime friend Rani Singh began the enormous task of gathering together the Harry Smith Archives, assembling his legacy, and sifting through the complicated and unlikely life Smith had led. A grant from the Grateful Dead's Rex Foundation allowed Smith to live the last few years of his life in a productive and, for Smith, relatively stable manner.

After the *Anthology* was reissued on CD, Smith received a Grammy in 1991 for lifetime achievement. Smith would die later that year, but ascending the steps to the stage in a tuxedo must have seemed to him a transcendent moment.

I'm glad to say that my dreams came true, he told the audience. I lived to see the world changed through music.

He was eulogized at his memorial by the likes of Dave Van Ronk and Ed Sanders of the Fugs, but the memorial that will always be around is the *Anthology* itself. Smith had set out to document the past, but in the end it seems not a replica but the living past itself.

YOU WOULDN'T STEAL THIS RECORD, Greil Marcus wrote famously in a review, establishing once and for all the criteria by which greatness is judged. A great record is one you'd steal if you couldn't get it any other way.

People steal *David Johansen and the Harry Smiths.* In less than a year I've lost eight or ten copies. I'll take the jewel box down from the shelf, and it's empty. It was there a week ago. I'll loan a copy to a friend, and another friend will take it from him. Either the disc contains some marvelous new encoding that causes it to vanish after an arbitrary number of plays, or once they hear it, people just have to possess this record.

It was at the University of Minnesota that I first heard about the Johansen record. A professor of American literature was talking about Harry Smith and his folk anthology. You've got to hear this album by David Johansen and the Harry Smiths, the professor said.

This seemed something of a non sequitur. I thought of the New York Dolls. I thought of Buster Poindexter. I don't think so, I said.

But he wouldn't have it. He was a convert, a true believer. He was washed in the blood. He drove us across Minneapolis to a record shop called the Electric Foetus.

Got that new David Johansen? he asked a clerk.

Right over there, the clerk said, pointing, as if an unknown record on an unknown label was as common as locating a loaf of bread in a convenience store. The professor paid for the record and handed it to me, a faintly superior expression on his face as if he knew something I didn't.

He did.

From the first notes of the first song it was apparent this wasn't a mere tribute album. I recalled Elvis Presley being quoted as saying: I don't sound like nobody. There was an almost eerie connection to Rabbit Brown, whose song "James Alley Blues" is covered, but Johansen didn't sound like nobody either.

They sit regarding you from a black-and-white photo on the cover of their first album, *The New York Dolls*, with expressions that vary from simpers to cold stares. The five young men seated on the sofa are dressed in what looks like thrift-shop hooker garb, and they are pancaked and rouged and lipsticked, the square root of decadence. David Johansen is the one in the middle: huge, dark bouffant and platform shoes, mouth a painted Cupid's bow.

Over all, the photograph is a sneer, an upraised middle finger that says, *I don't give a goddamn what you think.* They're going the Stones one better, not androgynous like Bowie or effeminate like Elton John but into some whole new territory. All in all they look just the way David Johansen says he wanted them to look: sixteen and bored shitless.

This is all geared to shock, or at least it was in 1973, when the album was released. The Dolls need to be taken in the context of 1973: the Eagles are flying over *Hotel California,* Bruce Springsteen was gearing himself up to be the future of rock n' roll, his *Time* and *Newsweek* covers already on the horizon. The Dolls even shocked New York a little, very briefly. New York is notoriously hard to shock.

The music on the album is the aural equivalent of the cover, defiant and clarifying, an inside joke that says, There's something happening here, and we don't care if you know what it is or not. Flailing guitars and drums and an out-of-step bass kick in at ninety miles an hour and then accelerate in little two-minute concertos that sound like the early Stones bereft of all restraints and social concerns and literary pretensions. They sound like elevated trains and car collisions in which folks perish, the neon cacophony of New York at night, the world ending not with a whimper but in a bedlam of rending crashes.

Johansen says the idea of the Dolls was to take music away from the recording studios and give it back to the kids, to make a sort of homemade music that anyone could do. That's a valid idea, a kid can't go out to the garage with three chords and a guitar and come up with *Sgt. Pepper's Lonely Heart's Club Band* or *Smiley Smile*. The New York Dolls put it within reach, and at the same time added the kick of rebellion that has fueled rock since the days of Jerry Lee Lewis and Little Richard.

For a giddy moment in the early 70s, the New York Dolls were at the cutting edge of rock music. Pursued by record companies and lionized by the Gotham underground and the rock critic literati simultaneously, Johansen and the Dolls seemed on the verge of stardom. They even fell in with a London fashion designer named Malcolm McLauren. He wanted to take them to England and outfit them in red patent leather. When the project fell through, McLauren returned to his native land and invented the Sex Pistols.

The Dolls recorded two albums. Neither sold very well, but they altered forever the idea of what a rock band could look and sound like. The Dolls were gone as suddenly as if they'd self-combusted. They left the field to imitators like Kiss, who refined the idea of dressing up and went on to make millions.

Johansen resurfaced as a solo singer-songwriter in the early 80s. His songwriting had improved, and his gruff post-Dylan voice stood out from the other folkies, but these records didn't do much either, though they did manage to build on the cult audience of fans and critics he'd carried away from the Dolls. Then he reinvented himself once again. This time the mask was that of Buster Poindexter, a pompadoured lounge singer performing with a swing band. Though Johansen had never followed trends, just his own interests and obsessions, this time they coincided with popular taste. Buster Poindexter struck a chord with the audience somehow, and the persona lives on to this day, when, almost by popular demand, Johansen resurrects Buster at clubs or private parties.

You have to eat, Johansen says dismissively of Buster, but the sound he came up with, a sort of blues-Latin-swing combination, predated the swing revival of the 90s and the work of musicians like Brian Setzer by almost a decade.

When Allan Pepper, owner of the Bottom Line, the legendary New York club, was preparing to celebrate the club's twenty-fifth anniversary, he asked Johansen to perform. But he wanted someone other than Buster Poindexter.

Al had been reading some books about Harry Smith, Johansen says. And I'd gone back and listened to the *Anthology*, and this four-volume collection from Shanachie called *Times Ain't Like They Used to Be.*

Depression-era stuff, really rural. And I got interested in this kind of stuff all over again.

Music has always been a part of Johansen's life, one of the earliest things he remembers. His father was a lover of opera, and he heard a lot of that, but early on, Johansen formed an attachment to old acoustic blues, later widening his appreciation to take in the electric-urban recordings of Muddy Waters and B.B. King and Sonny Boy Williamson. Around the age of fifteen he taught himself harmonica and guitar (I'm still almost as good now as I was then, he says today), which may seem a little unusual for a kid raised in New York City, but the usual has never been what Johansen does.

So for the Bottom Line gig he put together a band with this sort of music in mind: Guitarists Brian Koonin and Larry Saltzman together with bassist Kermit Driscoll and drummer Joey Baron. He had his blues band. Johansen professes to see not much of a stretch between them and the New York Dolls. The Dolls were a blues band, he insists. We just massacred the form. The bass player couldn't breathe and play at the same time. He'd take these big breaths and hold them and shoot out all these notes. Then he'd have to stop playing to breathe. It just happens that we can do both at the same time.

The show at the Bottom Line was supposed to be a onetime thing, but everything fell together. A write-up in the *New York Times* caused a lot of interest in the band, and besides, Johansen says, it was a lot of fun.

Norman Chesky, who had known Johansen from his Poindexter days and who owns Chesky records, a label known mainly for the intense quality of its recordings and for the mixture of ethnic, blues, and jazz releases, wanted to make a record with him.

During a three-day session at New York's St. Peter's Episcopal Church, the band, now calling themselves the Harry Smiths, recorded twenty-five songs. Thirteen of them made it onto the album.

The result was nothing short of a revelation. The record sounds at once timeless and state-of-the-art, like an Alan Lomax field recording made on some black sharecropper's front porch using marvelous equipment that did not yet exist. Johansen chose some of the songs from Smith's *Anthology* and others of the same somber shading.

I just did songs I like, Johansen says. It's a pretty dark record, usually someone expires in each of the songs.

The album was well reviewed everywhere from *Entertainment Weekly* to *Rolling Stone* to audiophile magazines like *Hi-Fi News*, and ultimately the British music publication *Mojo* would select it as one of the ten best blues albums of the year.

The general tone of the reviews was that a cross-dressing New York Doll had reinvented himself as a lounge singer and then again as an eighty-year-old bluesman, but Johansen is complicated and intelligent, and the truth is not quite that simple. A couple of the songs are staples from the Buster Poindexter days, and one of them, Sonny Boy Williamson's "Don't Start Me Talking", turned up on the Dolls' second album. Johansen has always been a marvelous actor, from his Doll days up through the films he's appeared in (such as *200 Cigarettes* and *Scrooged*), but there the seams fade and edges blur, and it is difficult to tell the actor from the man, the singer from the song, and that is the quality that the old alchemist Harry Smith was fascinated with.

You could see it as simply a matter of role-playing, of alternating one mask for another. But there's never the impression of the Manhattan skyline double-imaged onto a landscape of Mississippi Delta farmland.

The songs on *David Johansen and the Harry Smiths* are not note-for-note recreations, as the New Lost City Ramblers were wont to do, nor are they old songs reworded and modernized, made more accessible by the use of contemporary arrangements and the hewing off of rough edges, as Bill Morrissey did on his album of Mississippi John Hurt songs, or Dave Alvin did on his *Public Domain*.

He seems to work in the way some of the singers on the *Anthology* do, not interpreting the song or reinventing it but *inhabiting* it.

His take on "Oh Death" is like a cold, damp wind blowing off the river Styx. More chilling than the Ralph Stanley version on *O Brother, Where Art Thou?* soundtrack, it evokes the 1927 Dock Boggs performance, then edges it with a deeper shade of black. The voice sounds at an absolute remove from hope or life, and salvation is not even a consideration. Johansen sounds as if he has hellhounds on his trail and the Grim Reaper peering through the bedroom window, bone fingers already reaching to close his eyes and wire his jaws shut.

When asked about this quality, Johansen mentions darkness and light. Without dwelling on the darkness he was in (this was a guy, after all, who lived the life of a rock star) or the light he sees now, he says, You can be in the darkness and come into the light. But even though you're in the light, you know the darkness is still out there.

Johansen played some gigs in London earlier this year, just a bluesman sitting on a stool and cradling a guitar with a harmonica brace hung around his neck. It was a far cry from the way he looked in the early days. He had grown a beard, and he was wearing a plain, dark suit. He warned New York Dolls fans to stay away, nevertheless, old Dolls covers like "Don't Start Me Talking" got the most applause. But in London as well as New York, audiences seem perfectly comfortable with Johansen as a sort of method actor of the blues, and *Mojo* magazine said they had just seen a man who would go down in the books as being as artistically honest and creatively daring as the deceased bluesmen he now honors.

Like the tricksters and masked marvels and shape-shifters that populate the *Anthology*, both Harry Smith and David Johansen have an affinity for morphing roles and presenting an ever-changing façade to the world and, like the songs themselves, an aversion to being categorized or pinned down. They also share the music, for that is the glue that binds them together.

Time done been won't be no more, Furry Lewis warns in his version of "See That My Grave Is Kept

Clean", not only singing it but prefacing it with an imperative: Listen, he sings, as if he wants you to remember it, listen. Time done been won't be no more.

But in a sense, if a moment of time is the world we inhabit in that moment, it is the world that matters and not the clock that measures it.

In the end Johansen's music seems to be saying that the world doesn't change, only the guises it goes under, only the masks it wears.   Appearance is nothing. The essentials remain.   Love is still love, and loss is still loss.   Death was ever death and will remain so.   The dark is as black as it ever was, and the light is what you struggle toward, and that seems to matter as much to David Johansen as it did to Rabbit Brown or Harry Smith.

I BELIEVE I'LL BUY ME
A GRAVEYARD OF MY OWN

WHEN FURRY LEWIS WAS REDISCOVERED in Memphis in 1959 by Sam Charters, nothing much happened. The folk revival, when scholars and musicologists and collectors of worn 78 records on strange labels like Black Patti and Okeh would prowl Mississippi back roads looking for the old men who long ago recorded the music that was strange as the labels, did not come along until the early 60s. When it did, bluesmen like Mississippi John Hurt and Son House and Furry Lewis found themselves on the road again, playing to new audiences at the Newport Folk Festival and the East Coast coffeehouse circuit. Those old country-blues songs that had been dismissed, almost forgotten, were popular again.

Furry was born Walter Lewis in that fabled, near-mythic birthplace, and graveyard, of the blues, Greenwood, Mississippi. Just when is a matter of conjecture, Lewis was prone to altering his past history to suit the needs of the moment (he asserted that he invented the bottleneck style of guitar-playing that Robert Johnson used and that he was a protégé of W.C. Handy). The consensus is that he was born in 1893.

He didn't tarry long in Greenwood. His family moved to Memphis when he was seven years old. Before he was out of school, he was playing with folks who would one day be hailed as Beale Street legends: Will Shade, the Memphis Jug Band, and Handy, the man credited with igniting the first blues craze.

Furry was soon touring Arkansas and Mississippi with the medicine shows that were prevalent in the rural South of that time. By his teens, he was playing the jukes with Memphis Minnie and Blind Lemon Jefferson. He claimed to have learned the rudiments of guitar as a child from a street musician known to him only as Blind Joe. The rest he learned on his own, writing original songs in a tablet, and recasting ragtime pieces and popular songs with lines from the stockpile of interchangeable blues poetry that has been dipped into by everyone from Jimmie Rodgers to Bob Dylan.

In the late 1920s, Furry recorded twenty-three songs. Thus, Furry was squarely part of the 1927-29 historical musical outpouring that was probably the richest period in American recording. Men like Ralph Peer were scouring the South for talent, but no one had yet figured out what would sell and what wouldn't. The playing field was momentarily level and everyone had a shot, black bluesmen from the Delta and white string bands from the Carolinas, Georgia, and West Virginia. At least until the Great Depression hit and the record business nearly stopped, and then many musicians went back to doing what they were doing before.

What Furry had been doing before, aside from making music, was working for the city of Memphis. Despite losing a leg in a railroad accident in 1917 (doctors had replaced it with a wooden stump), Lewis got employment in 1922 as a street sweeper, a job he would hold off and on for the next forty-four years.

Those twenty-three recorded songs formed the strongest part of Furry's musical legacy. Mostly based on the twelve-bar blues pattern and played in open tunings, his songs featured familiar blues motifs that bobbed in and out like debris in turbulent waters, railroads and highways, cops and authority, empty beds, women who cling too tightly or won't hold on at all and all shot through with sardonic humor and violence that lies around the next bend in the road.

"I believe I'll buy me a graveyard of my own", he sings in *Furry's Blues*, his tone confiding, as if he's passing on hard-won knowledge, "I'm gonna kill everybody that have done me wrong."

Impending violence fuels his songs. Frustration and anger seethe just under the surface and there is a feeling that things could go south at a moment's notice. "If you want to go to Nashville men and they ain't got no fare", he sings, "Cut your good girl's throat and the judge will send you there". When things get too heavy, there's dark humor: I went down to the I.C. train, laid my head on the I.C. tracks, he sings in "Cannon Ball Blues". Seen the I.C. comin', Lord, and I snatched it back.

Furry's masterpiece is Kassie Jones, a long, imaginative reworking of the traditional song about the death of engineer Casey Jones in a 1900 train wreck in Canton, Mississippi. But Furry makes it his own, literally. The song begins typically enough with an account of

Casey as a folk hero, but takes a trip to the surreal when Furry himself emerges as a character: chased to his woman's gate by the police, welcomed to her folding bed, then on the road again, his name on the back of his shirt, "he's a natural-born easeman don't have to work."

Driven by Furry's hypnotic percussive bass strings, the song sounds like something Sam Phillips would have recorded at Sun Studio thirty years later.

In the 1970s, age had enfeebled his musicianship to the point that he was forced to get by on the tricks and showmanship of his medicine-show days, but, paradoxically, a brief fame touched him. In 1975, he opened in Memphis for the Rolling Stones, and in 1976 Joni Mitchell wrote "Furry Sings the Blues" about him. He even appeared in a movie that stars Burt Reynolds, W.W. and the Dixie Dancekings.

Furry had attended John Hurt's funeral in Greenwood, and most of the other country bluesmen were in the ground, too. By the time of his death in 1981, he had outlived most of his contemporaries. The strife and hard times Furry had written about were still around but they were being addressed by a different kind of music. The blues had gone Big City, and the acoustic country blues were practiced mostly by purists and academicians.

Maybe Furry himself said it best in his re-working of "St. Louis Blues": "Time done been/Won't be no more".

THE BANJO MAN

WHEN EMISSARIES OF THE BBC showed up at the Ryman Auditorium in 1946 to record performances by country musicians, no doubt to allow perplexed Londoners back home to hear what the rustic folks in the colonies considered entertainment. One of the first musicians they spotlighted was the Dixie Dewdrop. That would be Uncle Dave Macon, David Harrison Macon from Rutherford County, Tennessee, already seventy-six years old in 1946 and as unlikely a superstar as country music has ever seen.

But no one at the Opry was surprised. How could they not have chosen him? Who could compare to Uncle Dave? Macon in full-tilt abandon was like a natural force unleashed, and when he got unwound and release arrived it would be like watching destruction from the eye of a hurricane. He buckdanced and flashed his gold-toothed grin and twirled his banjo like a baton, brought it to his shoulder with the neck pointed at the audience and sprayed notes like a musical Gatling gun. His stamping and percussive rapping on his instrument rendered the idea of a rhythm section laughable: you couldn't duplicate this pandemonium, any effort would be the palest echo of the seemingly infinite energy he expended. Uncle Dave must have been hard on banjos.

He had arrived at the Ryman by a circuitous route, and in his quieter moments of reflection, late at night and winding down and alone in the Nashville Hotel where he finished out his days, he must have pondered the string of coincidences and singularities that had moved his life in so peculiar a direction.

Macon traveled a path that was to become familiar to the rural musicians who made it to the recording studios in the late 1920s their names are legion. But that path is now lost, it was unique to its time and place and simply does not exist anymore, no one will travel it again.

The Macons were a prosperous family before the Civil War. They owned upward of two thousand acres and various businesses, including distilleries and sawmills. But the cards fell wrong for prosperous farmers in the South, and by the time David Harrison Macon was born in 1870, things weren't looking so optimistic. Yankee Reconstruction had its foot on the region's neck and was pushing hard. Dave's father, John, struggled until 1883, and then decided, like a lot of other folks, that better times lay in the cities instead of the hardscrabble countryside. So he sold the house and what was left of the land, far fewer than two thousand acres, and loaded furniture and children onto the wagon, hitched up the mules, and started out the long sixty miles to Nashville. Dave was thirteen years old.

They went into the hotel business, and this, in retrospect, looks like the making of Uncle Dave the entertainer. The place they ran was the Broadway House. This was a time when a motley of entertainers would play the line of theaters on Broadway in downtown Nashville, and all these traveling performers had to stay somewhere. A lot of them chose the Broadway House, partly because they could use the huge open basement for rehearsals. These were performers of various stripes, jugglers and acrobats and musicians and magicians, animal acts and blackface minstrels and rube comedians.

These were also the days when audiences demanded showmanship. They'd come to be entertained, to be taken out of the ordinariness of their lives for the duration of the show, and they would settle for nothing less. Style weighed as heavily as content. Incertitude rang hollow, and mediocre showmen didn't last too long. Dave saw a lot of rehearsals, and he was soaking up influences from all of them.

About this time a circus turned up in Nashville and pitched its tents in a vacant field. There Macon saw a comedian banjoist named Joel Davidson. The experience must have been revelatory, for Macon himself later wrote, in the often overblown language of the times:

> *It was Joel Davidson who proved to be the spirit that touched the mainspring of the talent that inspired Uncle Dave to make his wishes known to his dear old mother and she gave him the money to purchase his first banjo.*

By 1887 all this had changed by a pocket knife: Macon's father lay dead in a street altercation and the trial ended in an acquittal for the assailant. Soon the family had abandoned Nashville and the widow Macon headed them for Readyville, a town between McMinnville and Murfreesboro where there was a waystation for stage coaches. She figured that travelers would always need food and a place to sleep. Essentially, they were still in the hotel business.

It is probably here that the idea of becoming a professional musician first entered young Dave's mind, for he built a makeshift stage atop a barn from which he could give impromptu shows for the travelers who were staying over. One can imagine this: a teenage boy with his open backed banjo and apparently boundless confidence, the end of the day and a skeptical crowd, Dave up there in the falling dark tuning his banjo while the nighthawks dart and check, the audience gauging him and Dave gauging them right back, trying to figure what will work and what won't for an embryonic repertoire he doesn't even know he needs yet.

All this time he kept learning songs, collecting them, writing them, stealing them. He also developed a distinctive introductory roll, almost like an invitation, a quiet caesura before the action starts, a musical hand gesturing you inside the song where the story commences, that would kick off most of his later songs.

At the age of twenty-nine, Dave married Matilda Richardson, who over the next twenty years would bear him seven sons. In 1900, with a child on the way, he looked about for a way to make a living. Ever a mule man, he went into the freight business. With a double team of mules, he hauled wagonloads of provisions and building materials and whiskey into towns the railroads did not accommodate. He was barely ahead of the internal combustion engine, but he wasn't put off by its arrival. He didn't trust the horseless carriage and he didn't expect it to last. In "From Earth to Heaven", a song he wrote about the freight business, he sings: "I'll bet a hundred dollars to a half a ginger cake/I'll be here when the trucks is gone".

When he became a more prolific writer of protest songs, this was a theme he returned to again and again: change is not always for the better, and change for the sake of change is never better. He seems like an early agrarian or one of Robert Penn Warren's Fugitives, trying to hold on to a mythic South that had been slipping through Southern fingers ever since the War. He believed in flesh and blood. He had more faith in a beast of burden he could talk to rather than some mechanical contrivance that would not do his bidding. In days to come he would own cars and even write a paean to Henry Ford's invention, but he never learned to drive one and he was always a little surprised when they performed as they were supposed to.

Now here's a stop on the road that doesn't exist anymore. Fiddlin' John Carson had a Victrola record released that sold way beyond expectations. It was the first country-music hit. Folks scraped up the money to buy it and hoped later they could scrape up the money to buy a phonograph to play it on. It seemed an occasion of country people embracing one of their own who'd in some manner made good and transcended them but managed to keep intact the roots they held in common.

The record companies were amazed, but they were not stupid. They began to look around for other rural musicians.

Records were largely a sideline then, carried in furniture stores rather than music shops. The Sterchi brothers owned a chain of furniture stores that carried a line of Vocalion recordings. Dave had hauled a lot of furniture, and by now he was the best-known musician in the region. He'd been performing informally (one can't imagine a formal performance by Uncle Dave Macon) for years at dances and private parties or wherever anybody wanted to hear a banjo played. He even had a partner now, a young man named Sid Harkreader who played guitar and fiddle and sang harmony with him. So when Vocalion asked the Sterchi brothers to help line up new talent, the first name out of the hat was Dave Macon's.

It must have been a potent moment: he'd been making music for free all his life and now he had the chance to perhaps get paid for it and lay everything else aside. But he was already fifty-three years old, a little late in life to be changing careers. But there seemed little choice. The freight business he knew had been supplanted by automobiles and he still had children at home to feed. He signed with Vicalion and headed for New York, not knowing that he was blazing a trail that countless musicians would follow: Jimmie Rodgers and the Carter Family, Dock Boggs and Mississippi John Hurt, plus scores of others whose epitaphs are just names on old phonograph records.

His first recording was "Keep My Skillet Good and Greasy", a song that in later years he would say he learned from a black man named Tom Davis, but history has forgotten Davis's story and no one knows where he learned it or how close to the original (if such a thing exists) Macon's version is. By making it his first record, Macon must have considered it his best shot at launching a new career and it is a song he returned to again and again and recorded numerous times, as if striving toward some ideal of musical perfection.

All the versions have the same feel of not only lost landscapes and lost times but a lost people, a race supplanted. The banjo rolls hollowly out and it seems to be coming from some place enormously distant, from some alternate world outside time itself, and the voice when it comes, conspiratorial and amused, jerks you abruptly into a plot that's already started: there's stolen meat in your knapsack, hounds on your track, and you're pulling for your shanty home where Mandy is waiting. The song is all motion and action, there's no time for rationalization or introspection but, above all, it is so caught up in the joy of life that everything else seems incidental.

In this song and in songs like "Way Down the Old Plank Road" and "Buddy Won't You Roll Down the

Line" (both included by Harry Smith, no slouch in taste, on his *Anthology of American Folk Music*), the music creates a visceral three-dimensional world then draws you in to a time that doesn't exist anymore but stills feels prescient. Times and circumstances alter, the music says, but the eternal human frailties and verities remain the same. There's always that sense of being vividly alive. In "Way Down the Old Plank Road", the feeling of desperate abandon when Macon cries KILL YOURSELF! sounds as if the words could be either a command or a mental note to himself. Hard times or good times, there is a stoic, dark-humored core that seems to render qualifiers or modifiers irrelevant. It is not the good times or the bad times that matter but the experience of living itself.

The reaction to these first recordings was immediate. There seemed to have been an audience already poised and waiting on Uncle Dave, and all that was needed was this connection to bind them together.

When he was booked into the Loews Theater in Birmingham, Alabama, there weren't enough seats for all the folks who wanted to sit in them. A two-week engagement extended to five, and still the place was packed. The theater manager was arrested by the fire marshal for permitting too many fans inside.

Soon Macon was playing the Loews chain from Boston to Florida and beyond. At an age when most men are contemplating retirement, Uncle Dave Macon was on the road to becoming country music's newest superstar.

Macon was far luckier than most: the crash of 1929 sent most rural musicians back to sharecropping and coal mining, but Macon had a job on the Grand Ole Opry, and he always had a label willing to release his music.

He wrote protest songs about prohibition (Dave took it personal that it had become so hard to buy a decent drink of whiskey), about the downtrodden farmer ("Eleven Cent Cotton"), and about whatever peeved him at the moment, always with a stoic humor that regarded the world with a sort of sardonic fatalism.

Time and Change–always Macon's enemies–were rolling on down the line. The Opry was big business. He had grown old, beginning to sound dated to more modern ears. The Young Turks of country music were coming aboard, and Macon regarded them with a jaundiced eye. To him, showmanship was half the music, and most of these trespassers came up wanting. They didn't have the requisite style. *You're a pretty fair banjo picker*, he told Earl Scruggs, *but you're not very funny.*

By the end of the 40s, the music was changing and the audience was changing with it. Hank Williams had arrived and country-music singers were beginning to be judged as sex idols the way that movie stars were. Macon's wife had died and he was spending lonesome nights in a Nashville hotel. Before he died in 1952, he willed one of his banjos to a young entertainer named Stringbean Akeman whom he considered his protégé, but he must have seen the time coming when clog-dancing banjo pickers would be reduced to comic relief between modern songs.

He couldn't have known the whole of it, the arrival in Nashville of a new breed of producers like Chet Atkins and Owen Bradley and crooners like Jim Reeves who sweetened the music and diluted it until it was more palatable to audiences with an affinity for mainstream pop. Perhaps he would have harkened back to his days with the showmen in the basement of the Broadway House and found it ironic that style was still supplanting substance, veneer more than ever disguising reality.

Even banjo-playing altered. There would come a time when newgrass pickers would try to force the banjo into the realm of quantum physics. But Macon's own playing was not as simple as it sometimes sounded. In his later days, nearing eighty, he relied mostly on a frailing or clawhammer technique, but scholars dissecting his 1920s recordings have identified almost a score of different styles that he had mastered running from ragtime to blues and they're still finding more. And any one of them sounds realer and truer than anything that has come along since.

HAND ME MY TRAVELING SHOES

NOT LONG AFTER BLIND WILLIE MCTELL graduated from the School for the Blind in Macon, Georgia, he turned up in Atlanta. (There's a theory that says he's Blind Willie McTear, that an instructor at the school misheard McTell and wrote the name down wrong, so perhaps the mythic weight of having your name committed to some sort of legal document in that time and place made you beholden not only to the authority that signed the papers and affixed seals of legality, but to the lesser authority that served and interpreted them.) Something was beginning to happen in American music, and a lot of it was happening in Atlanta. Street musicians dependent upon coins tossed in guitar cases or passed hats were drawn there by the city's size and relative prosperity. If you only counted the blind musicians and ignored the sighted, you'd still come up with an impressive number.

Truly there must have been giants on the earth in those days. All those blind blues singers were steady on the move, crisscrossing the South like black spores on a glass slide, setting up on street corners and opening their guitar cases, ears attuned for the clink of change, always alert for a new song they could borrow and make their own with lines from the floating debris of a thousand other blues songs. They lugged their guitars and coat-hanger harmonica racks, uncertain where they'd be when night fell on them, whose floor they'd sleep on, where the next meal was coming from and when it would get there. The corners on Decatur Street must have thronged with them, the competition for prime locations must have been fierce. Imagine the traffic jams, the fortunes a seeing-eye-dog franchise could have made. It was a harsh and provisional world McTell had come into. You had to be tough just to survive.

Dark was the night, cold was the ground. When Blind Willie Johnson turned up in Atlanta, McTell almost immediately hooked up with him. Johnson was a slide-guitar player of great technical proficiency, and he was also a Baptist minister, and between them they covered the field, both the secular and the washed in the blood.

Riley Puckett was there. He was a white guitarist (blind too, of course, and also working the streetcorners) who within a couple of years would play lead guitar with the Skillet Lickers, his innovative picking and odd bass runs helping the Skillet Lickers to sell a lot of records and making this white string band the Rolling Stones of their day. (Bootleggers rejoiced and laid on an extra shift when the Skillet Lickers came to Atlanta to record.)

A lot of things will remain mysterious about Blind Willie McTell, and not the least of them is whether or not he ever played with Puckett. But the odds are that they met. Some of the Skillet Lickers' recordings, like "Georgia Rag" and "Razor Ball", have the ragtimey feel of McTell songs, and there was at this time an enormous amount of cross-pollination going on in music. You are what you hear, perhaps. McTell's own music is more Piedmont than Mississippi Delta blues. His voice is higher and more nasal than the conventional blues singer's voice, and the music is more accessible than, say, Son House or Charley Patton. (Having recorded McTell, the archivist John Lomax initially declined to release the sessions. He had recorded McKinley Morganfield and Son House, and being more familiar with the traditional country blues sound, he complained that McTell did not sound enough like a blues singer.)

Of course, if you're playing for an audience and you expect to get paid, the idea is to play something the audience wants to hear. A background of performing in carnivals and tent shows and the picnics that at the time were part of the African-American social scene had given McTell's repertoire a broader sweep than most Bluesmen. Listening to his catalogue, you hear music that ranges from traditional twelve-bar blues to ragtime to sly, ribald songs that must have made him the life of the party, to songs that existed for no other reason than to allow him to do some virtuoso guitar-picking, and that hat must have come back heavy then. The conclusion that he knew what he was doing is incontestable.

McTell and Blind Willie Johnson traveled what was known as the Georgia circuit: Atlanta and Augusta, Savannah and Macon. Had they wandered south and stumbled across the fabled crossroads where a decade later Robert Johnson would deal with Satan, McTell might have bargained for his vision: he had been blind all his life and he could already play the guitar.

Still, he was luckier than most. He'd learned at the blind school in Macon not only to read words but to read music by feeling out the shape of the notes with his fingertips, in a time when even most sighted musicians learned and performed by ear. And he could take care of himself. He'd been a hard worker since his early teens, working with carnivals and traveling medicine shows and minstrel shows.

He was born in Thomson, Georgia, either in 1898 or 1901, depending on which source you want to believe. By the time the McTells (or McTears: there's another story that someone on the father's side of the family had changed the name from McTell because of trouble with whiskey stills and government revenuers) had moved to Statesboro, Willie had been shown the rudiments of guitar playing by his mother, and he gathered more skill from neighbors and visiting pickers and whomever he met, soaking it all up. Already he was writing songs in his head and changing other tunes to his liking and already he was developing an affinity for wandering, a habit that would stay with him all his days.

By the time he arrived in Atlanta, he'd also taken up the twelve-string guitar. He'd learned on the six-string, but had seen that for his purposes the twelve was infinitely better. With its complementary strings tuned an octave higher than the regular strings, not only was there more volume, but whether fingerpicking or using a bottleneck, the higher strings enriched the melody and elaborated on it. It also set him apart from other street musicians.

All these street pickers were living too close to the ground to know that they were part of the dawning of the richest, most complex period of American music. This period began around 1926 and would last only until the beginning of the Depression, and it would not come again.

Though McTell couldn't have known it, by 1926 the record business was turning toward him. The sales of phonograph records had grown exponentially, and things were to a point where there was a lot of money to be made. To the surprise of executives in New York, people in the rural South bought a lot of music. A record by a fiddle player named John Carson sold faster than Atlanta record stores could restock it. This was the sort of news that got noticed in New York. People so poor they sometimes had to choose between a phonograph record or a new pair of shoes were opting for the music, choosing the magic over the practical, the mystery and wonder of their lives encoded into spiraling grooves of shellac.

McTell sings in "Let Me Play with Yo' Yo-Yo":

> I'll take all my money
> put up against the wall
> I'll take what sticks
> and you can have what fall.

Record-company owners were doing essentially this very thing. They were in the process of figuring out what sold best, they had not yet learned how to homogenize and move it toward a one-size-fits-all center, so they were throwing everything at the wall.

A lot of weird music was sticking: like Frank Hutchison's bizarre take on the sinking of the Titanic, with do-si-do square dances being held on the lower decks and the captain inquiring, How's your machinery? Or Dick Justice's "Cocaine", its imagery and cast of characters, furniture repo men, whipped babies, and women in alleys, the narrator simply wild about his good cocaine making a sort of jagged, surreal poetry that would soon vanish from popular music and not come around again until Bob Dylan surfaced in the early 60s. The Okeh label was recording Dock Boggs, a Virginia coal miner whose dark music and eerie hollow banjo sounded like what you'd hear if you leaned your head against the door to hell to eavesdrop.

These three performers had in common not only that they were white, but the fact that they didn't much sound like it. All three were steeped in the blues, a variant of it that would come to be thought of as white or mountain blues. The record companies were also recording a Texan named Blind Lemon Jefferson and a street singer named Blind Blake, and in 1927 Victor got around to Blind Willie McTell.

For a blind man, McTell possessed an amazing degree of self-sufficiency. He figured out the intricacies of the New York subway system and got wherever he needed to be.

He recorded again in 1928, this time for Columbia, and these two sessions produced classic songs like "Broke Down Engine" and "Mama, Tain't Long Fo' Day" and "Statesboro Blues" that would roll down the years and resonate with musicians like the Allman Brothers and the White Stripes long after McTell was gone.

His song "Delia", a stoic, dark-humored account (took Delia to the graveyard, never brought her back) of a woman murdered by her lover (say you love them rounders, and don't love me), reads like an O'Connor story or E.A. Robinson poem. Dylan covered it in the early 90s. Johnny Cash rewrote it as "Delia's Gone", but he kept the song's air of detached, matter-of-fact violence.

Almost before it had begun, the boom was over. Something had fallen on Wall Street, folks said. Whatever had fallen, its echoes rippled on and on. The record business was hit hard, nowhere harder than in the rural South, sharecropper or millhand, black or white. First Reconstruction and now this Wall Street debacle. A choice between a new record and a little flour and lard is not really a choice.

Dock Boggs went back to the coal mines, Frank Hutchison went to work in a West Virginia grocery store, John Hurt went back to sharecropping in Mississippi. William Samuel McTell had nowhere to go except to the music he hadn't even left, so he went back to Decatur Street and wherever his traveling shoes and traveling blues would take him. In the early 30s, he sojourned all over the South with Blind Lemon Jefferson.

In 1934 he married Ruth Kate Williams, who long after McTell was dead would remember what he told her when she asked why he stayed on the road so much: "Baby, I was born a rambler. I'm gonna ramble until I die."

Listening through McTell's recorded work is almost like participating in a séance. Spirits come out of the dark, dead voices and the voices of folks not yet born when the recordings were made speak through the music, and amaze you at how much came from McTell.

The picking and strumming pattern he uses in songs like Mr. McTell's "Got the Blues" shows up in Jimmie Rodger's numbered blue yodels, and occasionally some of the words: *She's tailor made, she ain't no hand-me-down.* Eric Clapton uses the guitar lick and some of the words from "Stole Rider Blues" in his own "Motherless Child". Taj Mahal and the Allman Brothers put their own spin on Statesboro Blues". Any good gal's got a mojo but she's tryin' to keep it hid, he sings on "Scarey Day Blues", and over the years McTell had become adept at hiding his own mojo, swapping one mask for another, sliding adroitly from role to role as if simply changing clothes.

When word circulated that a new recording scout was in Atlanta, McTell immediately turned up with his guitar and a new persona, ready to make a record. He was Red Hot Willie Glaze for Bluebird. He was Blind Sammie for Columbia, and Georgia Bill for Okeh. He was also Blind Willie for Vocalion, Barrelhouse Sammy, and naming himself after a barbecue joint where the tips had been good, he was Pig n' Whistle Red when he cut some sides for Regal.

When McTell was in his fifties he abruptly quit singing anything but spirituals. No more playful ribaldry like "Let Me Play with Yo' Yo-Yo", no more mojos Mama wouldn't let him see. In 1957 he began preaching in the Mt. Zion Baptist Church in Atlanta. Maybe he heard the sand running in the glass. His widow said in an interview in 1977 that he was tired, that he said he wanted to get back to God.

His last recording session took place a year before he laid it all aside to follow religion. A man named Ed Rhodes, who ran a record store in Atlanta, heard that there was a blind guitar player singing for tips behind a bar called The Blue Lantern Club, a musician playing the twelve-string guitar and sounding just like Huddie Ledbetter.

Rhodes went to see for himself. It was McTell, and Rhodes, who owned some recording equipment, tried to persuade McTell to record for him. Considering that he had recorded for decades under a dozen different names, McTell was strangely hesitant, but ultimately he was talked into it. Over a period of several weeks, McTell loosened up and reprised an entire career's worth of music. The songs were interspersed with accounts of his years on the road, an oral autobiography of his life and times.

Intentions here were good, the follow-through left much to be desired. The tapes languished for years in an attic, ultimately winding up in a garbage can. When they were discovered, only one salvageable reel of tape remained. (It was released on Prestige/Bluesville as Blind Willie McTell's *Last Session.)*

He'd long suffered from diabetes, and complications from the disease brought on a stroke. He died in 1959 in the state hospital in Milledgeville, Georgia. When he was buried outside Thomson, his tombstone read: WILLIAM McTEAR.

So he never lived to see the 60s, when the old blues giants were sought out and lionized, when necktied Yankees showed up on Mississippi John Hurt's front porch and waited for him to come in from the field. He never worked the college circuit like Son House and Brownie McGhee and Sonny Terry. When he died, the great folk revival was still embryonic, the Kingston Trio in matching blazers were singing antiseptic versions of Appalachian ballads. Yet to be were Dylan, Elizabeth Cotton's strung-upside-down guitar playing "Freight Train" on national television, Robert Johnson bubbling under Billboard's Hot 100.

Blind Willie McTell was in the ground but his music wasn't. Plunder his music and you'll find the bones of other music not fleshed out.

Dylan, in particular, has been instrumental in keeping McTell's music alive. He recorded respectful, loving versions of "Delia" and "Broke Down Engine". Perhaps part of Dylan's McTell attraction was the shifting personas, the Blind Sammies and Pig 'n' Whistle Reds. Dylan once recorded under the name of Blind Boy Grunt, and his own closets must be stuffed with masks he's cast off and disguises he's sent out to be altered again and again.

In 1983 Dylan wrote the ultimate eulogy, Blind Willie McTell, one of the most haunting songs, an impressionistic distillate of East Texas martyrs, Southern plantations burning,, the ghosts of slavery ships.

Between the lines you can imagine Blind Willie McTell and Blind Willie Johnson working that Atlanta, Augusta, Macon, Savannah circuit, traveling the dirt roads in the darkness they are heir to, a quarter moon unseen over the trees, their guitar cases carried like credit cards that will get them a meal, a pallet on the floor, a woman's smile they can feel rather than see, a poet's voice forty years down the line that will sing: *No one can sing the blues like Blind Willie McTell.*

Time Done Been Won't Be No More

SITTING ON TOP OF THE WORLD

THE WEEK BEFORE MERLEFEST I went by to check on Grady, and he was putting a fuel pump on his RV. It was a huge RV so ancient it looked like something the Joads might have fled the Dust Bowl in, and something was always going wrong with it. Grady had skinned knuckles and a half-drunk beer and a home-rolled Prince Albert cigarette stuck to his lower lip that waggled when he talked.

He was not in the best of moods.

I don't think I'm going to this one, he said. It's got to where all this traveling around costs too much money. I believe I've about seen everything anyway.

I looked at the RV. It was emblazoned with hand-painted legends memorializing bluegrass festivals past. The Bean Blossom Festival, the Foggy Mountain Festival, MerleFest '96, '97, '98. Maybe he *had* seen everything. He told me about Dylan at the 1964 Newport Folk Festival, cracking a bullwhip and preening as the newly crowned King of Folk. Another time at Newport, his RV had been parked next to the one belonging to Mother Maybelle Carter. They had sat in lawn chairs and watched twilight come on, and she had shown him how to play the autoharp, placing his fingers just so to form the chords.

Grady told me a lot of things, but he had the goods to back it all up. The walls of the house he rented were papered with surrealistic collages of photographs of the high and the mighty, the late and the great: Bill Monroe, the Stanley Brothers, Flatt and Scruggs, Don Reno and Red Smiley. Grady was in a lot of the pictures. Bill Monroe was embracing him like a long-lost brother in one, and there were pictures of Grady's own band, the Greenbriar Boys, skinny guys in Hank Williams suits standing before old-timey WSM microphones as if they were frozen back in the back and white 40s.

If you go, go up and talk to Doc Watson, Grady said.

I may. I always wanted to know where he got that arrangement for "Sitting on Top of the World". He got it off that old record by the Mississippi Sheiks.

I heard that record. That's not the arrangement.

Well, hell. Just go up and ask him. Walk right up to him, he'll tell you. He's not stuck up like a lot of them are. He's a hell of a nice guy.

Well, he's blind. Maybe that makes him a little more approachable.

Grady didn't want to hear it. A blind man can be a prick the same as anybody else, he said. He's just a hell of a nice guy.

Early in the morning of October 23, 1985, Arthel Doc Watson received the worst news a father can get. His son was dead. Eddy Merle Watson had been plowing on a steep hillside when the tractor he was driving overturned and rolled on him.

It was a blow that Doc almost did not recover from. It was a blow that resonated on a number of levels: aside from the incalculable loss of a child, Doc had lost a friend and a fellow musician. For a time it seemed he might even lose the music as well, because Merle and Doc and the music were inextricably bound together.

In 1964, when he was fourteen, Merle had learned to play guitar while his father was away. He had learned to play it so well that when Doc went back on the road, Merle went with him. That fall they played Berkeley Folk Festival, and he was all over the place on Doc's next album, *Southbound*. They toured and recorded together for the next twenty-one years, right up to that morning in 1985.

Merle became a proficient blues guitarist, and some of the albums subtly reflect his love for the genre. But he could pick flattop guitar with the best of them, and he could frail the banjo in the style of country performers like Uncle Dave Macon. When he died he was a few days away from winning *Frets* magazine's Bluegrass Picker of the Year award.

In what may be one of the few purely altruistic gestures in the music business, a handful of folks decided to do something. A friend of Doc's, Bill Young, together with Townes and Ala Sue Wyke, approached Doc with a proposition. Townes is Dean of Resource Development at Wilkes Community College, in Wilkesboro, North Carolina, and the three of them convinced Doc to play a benefit concert on the campus. The funds raised would be used to create a memorial garden in Merle's honor.

Doc agreed, and a few of Merle's friends, including the banjoist Tim O'Brien, volunteered their time and ended up playing from the beds of two flatbed trucks.

That was the first MerleFest, in 1988. By contrast, the festival in 1999, while still held on the college campus, was a vast sprawl of tents and stages and concessions accommodating more than a hundred performers and over sixty-two thousand people in the audience.

There was not a flatbed truck in sight.

The first night of the festival was cold and rainy, but the performances went on inside tents, where hundreds of folding chairs were arranged in rows. When you came out of the tents, the wind would be blowing and the rain would sting your face, but nobody seemed to mind. Earlier there had been a little grumbling when the performer list had been released: Hootie and the Blowfish? Steve Earle? These were not the direct descendants of Bill Monroe. Earle had been touring with the bluegrass great Del McCoury, but there was a loose-cannon quality about him, and he was a lot more edgy and confrontational than, say, Ralph Stanley.

But never mind. This audience could take it in stride. They had come to have a good time, and by God they were going to have a good time.

There is some kind of common bond between participant and observer, common heritage maybe, the unspoken reverence for certain values: family, home, and the tattered remains of the American Dream. Disparate elements of the audience mingled as easily as Freemasons meeting far from home and exchanging the password. Except here no password was needed. The fact that you were here seemed password enough.

The second day was sunny and as perfect as days in April get, and the shuttles were busy early ferrying folks down to the main gate. The parking lot is a mile or so from the festival, and buses carry festival-goers down a winding road to the entrance. Watching this potential audience disembark you are struck by the fact that there seems to be no type, no average, and that every spectrum of America is represented: middle-aged hippies and their new SUV driving yuppie offspring, farmers and farmers' wives, factory workers, the well-off in expensive outdoor gear from L.L. Bean, and longhaired young men in beards and fool's motley who seemed determined to be ready should the 60s clock around again.

And just as you are about to decide that there is no common element among the spectators, you notice the percentage of people carrying instruments. Guitars and banjos in hardshells. Cased fiddles tucked under the arm and God knows how many harmonicas pocketed like concealed weapons.

You don't see this at a rock concert or at the Grand Ole Opry, folks coming equipped to make their own music should the need arise. But bluegrass is widely perceived as handmade music, as opposed to, say, the output of song factories on Nashville's Music Row. The people who love bluegrass love it enough to learn to play it, and they are intensely loyal to the music, to the performers, and to one another. That love of music is the common factor, the source of the brotherhood that seems to radiate off the audience like good vibrations.

Music is always in the air here. Wandering past tents and the open-air stages, you hear it segue from bluegrass to old-time rustic to a tent where a Cajun saws his fiddle at breakneck speed, and young girls jerk and sway with their partners on sawdust-strewn floors. There are vendors everywhere. MerleFest is a growth industry. Attendance has grown every year that the festival has been in existence, but not as fast as the number of vendors and service providers: you can buy the usual tapes and CDs of your favorites, t-shirts and sweatshirts and blankets and plaster busts of musicians and folk art and homemade jewelry, Italian food and Mexican food and down-home American food, anything you want to drink, unless you want it to contain alcohol, alcohol is forbidden on the festival grounds.

During the course of the four-day festival, you learn that a lot of these people know one another. They know one another well enough to remember the names of their respective children and what everybody does for a living. They will meet again before the year is out, whether they live in Alabama or Pennsylvania. They begin in the spring, at MerleFest, and through the careful allocation of vacation days or the advent of three-day weekends, their paths will cross at bluegrass festivals in the South, or in Midwestern states like Michigan or Indiana, where bluegrass is almost a religion. They will see the shows and late in the day will get together and grill out and catch up on old times. Likely they will drink a beer or two and make a little music themselves.

Like family. In a sense they are a family, loose and nomadic but keeping in touch, and at the very bottom of this family is what they believe bluegrass music is all about.

Family and Doc Watson

Doc Watson, blinded by an eye infection during infancy, first learned to play the harmonica. From there he went to a banjo with a drum made from the skin of a house cat. But when he'd listen to records, the guitar was what he liked, and he began fooling around with one his brother had borrowed. His father heard Doc and told him that if he could learn a song by the end of the day, then he would buy Doc one of his own. When his father came in from work that night, Doc played "When Roses Bloom in Dixieland", and the next day Doc owned his first guitar.

Watson was playing on the radio at age nineteen, and in the years between learning that first song and becoming an icon, he played roadhouses and church socials and square dances. He played all kinds of music, country, rockabilly, swing, Appalachian ballads about young women wronged by their lovers.

It is amazing to listen to the Folkways records Doc made with Clarence Tom Ashley in the early days of the 60s. His style seems fully formed: the complex picking, the impeccable interaction between bass and treble strings, the breathless, death-defying runs he interjects into spaces of time so small there seems scarcely room to accommodate them. You keep listening for him to miss a note, deaden a string, but he does not. There have been countless long and drunken arguments over how many guitars, one or two, were playing on a particular track. It was one guitar, Doc's guitar.

In every great performer's life there are watershed concerts, events that forever alter the rest of the career from what has gone before. For Doc one of these came in 1963, when he was brought to the Newport Folk Festival by the folklorist Ralph Rinzler. Doc was forty-one years old. He sang about blackberry blossoms, shady groves, houses of the rising sun, and the sad fatalism of sitting on top of the world. When he began, he was an unknown guitarist with a pleasant baritone, on a long and winding road from Deep Gap, North Carolina. When he was helped from the chair and led from the stage, he was on his way to a contract with Vanguard Records, and he had reinvented forever the way folk musicians approached the guitar.

As has been said, there are more than a hundred performers here, and there are no slouches. These are the heavy hitters and brand-name pickers of bluegrass, everyone from hardshell traditionalists to the avant-garde, folks who through virtuoso playing and infusions from jazz are moving bluegrass into new and uncharted territory.

But no one questions what this thing is all about.

The Texas singer-songwriter Guy Clark usually performs his song "Dublin Blues" during his sets, a song that has the quatrain:

> I have seen the *David*
> I've seen the *Mona Lisa* too
> I have heard Doc Watson
> Play Columbus Stockade Blues

At the mention of Watson's name there is an outbreak of applause, thunderous and spontaneous. It happens the same way before different audiences each time Clark performs the song.

When Doc is led up the wooden steps to the stage, he approaches from the rear, and the first thing you see is his silver hair. At the first sight of it, the audience erupts. Doc is guided across the stage to where folding chairs have been positioned before the microphones. He is assisted into a chair, and he feels for the guitar in the open case beside his seat. He takes the guitar and sits cradling it, his face turned toward the crowd he can feel but not see, waiting until the applause dies down.

A stocky young man with a black beard has seated himself in the chair beside Doc's. He has taken up a guitar as well. He touches Watson's arm, and Watson leans toward the microphone.

This is my grandson Richard, he says, and he's going to help me out a little here. This is Merle's boy.

The crowd erupts again. The torch has been passed.

Doc's guitar kicks off a set of country blues, old Jimmie Rodgers songs, and the song Clark referenced. The third generation holds his own with ease, as if perhaps guitar playing was simply a matter of genetics.

Between songs Doc jokes easily with the audience, tells a couple of stories. The audience eats it up. They're eager to laugh at his stories, and maybe they've heard them before, their laughter anticipates the punch lines. They love him. He could sell them a used car with a blown transmission, a refrigerator that keeps things warm instead of cold. His voice is comforting and reassuring. He could be a neighbor sitting on the edge of your porch, or rocking right slow in the willow rocker.

Except for the playing. The picking is impeccable, it's what you expect Doc to do: the hands sure and quick, the notes clean and distinct, and the absolute right note to go where he picks it. Those cannot be seventy-six-year-old hands, the audience is thinking.

Maybe they are not of a mortal at all, maybe they are the hands of a king, a god.

And with the guitar clasped to him and his fingers moving over the strings, he is a god, the king of what he does. They are the hands of a man sitting on top of the world.

But every set has to end, and when this one does, and Doc begins to rise, his hand reaching for the hand that without seeing he knows is reaching for his own, and the hands touch, the illusion shatters: the audience sees that he is not a god at all but a mortal with frailties like the rest of us, and this somehow is more endearing yet.

The applause erupts again.

Chet Atkins is the best guitar player in the world, Doc said.

I figured you'd say Merle Travis.

Well, Merle was a great influence on me. I named (my son) Merle after him, and we finally met when we did that *Will the Circle Be Unbroken* record. But Chet's the best. He can play anything.

That's what people say about you, I said.

I'm slowing down a little. I'm getting older, and I can feel my hands stiffening up. I don't tour as much as I used to. I can feel myself slowing down, some of the runs are slower.

Close-up, Watson's face is pleasant, ruddy, the silver hair a little thin but waved neatly back, every strand in place. He does not wear dark glasses, as most blind performers do, and in fact, it is easy to forget that he is blind. The lids are lowered, the eyes just slits, and he looks almost as if he's just squinting into strong sunlight.

Where'd you come up with the picking on "Sitting on Top of the World"?

Watson laughed. I made that up, he said, that's my arrangement. I heard it off that old Mississippi Sheiks record. You might not have heard of them. But I changed it. I just played it the way I wanted it.

What do you think about the way MerleFest has grown? It's pretty big business now.

Well, it's good for the music. It's good for Merle, to keep people thinking about him. And people have to make a living, have to sell records. It's good to know so many people love this kind of music enough to come way down here to hear it.

Do you think it's changing? Music, I mean?

Music is always changing, Doc said. But it's all music, just people getting together and playing. One thing I noticed though, somebody told me there were some complaints about one of the performers using some pretty rough language over the mic during his show. I don't care for that. This has always been a family thing, women and kids, and that young fellow needs to remember where he is.

It was almost dark, and gospel music was rising from the tents when I walked down the road toward the parking lot. It was Sunday, the last day of the festival, and gospel was mostly what today had been about. There had been Lucinda Williams, of course, but mostly it had been gospel, like Sundays on old-time radio when the Sabbath was a day of respite from the secular.

Off to the right were the campgrounds. You could see the RVs, but they were hazy and ambiguous through the failing light, and music was rising from there too, the plinking of a banjo, a fiddle sawing its way through some old reel.

What you could see best were the campfires scattered across the bottomland, and for an illusory moment, time slipped, and it could have been a hobo camp or a campground for Okies on their way to the Golden State. There was a gully beyond the camp area. It was shrouded with trees, and fog lay between the trees like smoke, and it was easy to image Tom Joad slipping through them like a wraith, fleeing the vigilante men on his way upstate to organize the orange pickers. Or Woody Guthrie himself might ease up out of the fog, his fascist-killing guitar strung about his neck, a sly grin on his face that said all the world was a joke and only he was in on it. He'd warm his hands over the fire, for the night had turned chill, and he'd drink a cup of chicory coffee before heading down one of those long, lonesome roads Woody was always heading down.

Then I was closer, and I saw that the fires were charcoal and gas grills, where ground beef sizzled in tinfoil, and hot dogs dripped sputtering grease, and I saw that these people were much too affluent to be Okies and that the guitars they played were Fenders and Gibsons and Martins. They were guitars that Woody would never have been able to afford.

After a while Grady wandered up. I knew he'd made it, since I'd seen him a couple of times in crowds and had seen him playing guitar in a tent with other players, guys with homemade basses and washboards and

Jew's harps and whatever fell to hand. I hadn't talked to him yet, though.

You learn what you wanted to know?

Doc heard it off that old Mississippi Sheiks record, I said.

I told you that.

He invented the arrangement, though. It's his song now.

But he did talk to you. Was I right about him, or not?

I guess you were right, I said.

I thought about it. It seemed to me that Doc embodied the kind of values that are going out of style and don't mean as much as they used to: self-respect and respect for others, the stoic forbearance that Walker Evans photographed and James Agee wrote poems about. Something inside that was as immutable and unchanging as stone, that after a lifetime in show business still endured, still believed in the sanctity of womanhood, family, property lines, the church in the wildwood, the ultimate redeemability of humankind itself.

Life sometimes seems choreographed from the stage of a talk show, where barbaric guests haul forth dirty linen and a barbaric audience applauds, where presidents disassemble themselves before a voyeuristic media, where folks sell their souls to the highest bidder and then welsh on the deal. It was nice that Doc was still just being Doc, just being a hell of a nice guy.

But Doc's getting old, and those values are getting old, too. Maybe they're dying out. Maybe in the end there will just be the music. For there will always be the music. It is what Doc loves above all things: from show tunes like "Summertime" to music leaked up through time from old, worn 78's by Mississippi string bands, from the hollow, ghostly banjo of Dock Boggs to the contemporary folk of writers like Tom Paxton and Bob Dylan.

All music that will endure and help us endure. The music will never let you down.

Time Done Been Won't Be No More

BIBLIOGRAPHY

NOTE: The "Bibliography" does not include all of William Gay's shorter reviews, liner notes or other miscellaneous prose. Everything in the book, except for the excerpt from *The Lost Country*, has been previously published. The "Bibliography" indicates the first publication of each of the other pieces included in this book.

Time Done Been Won't Be No More

NOVELS

The Long Home, MacMurray and Beck, Denver, CO, 1999
The Long Home, Faber and Faber, London, England, 1999
Provinces of Night, Doubleday, New York, NY, 2000
Provinces of Night, Faber and Faber, London, England, 2000
Provinzen der Nacht, Argon Verlag GmbH, Berlin, Germany, 2001
Twilight, MacAdam/Cage, San Francisco, CA, 2006
Twilight, Faber and Faber, London, England, 2007
The Lost Country, Forthcoming

NOVELLAS

The Paperhanger, the Doctor's Wife and the Child Who Went into the Abstract, The Book Source, Hohenwald, TN, 1999
Come Home, Come Home, It's Suppertime, The Book Source, Hohenwald, TN, 2000

SHORT STORY–COLLECTIONS

I Hate to See that Evening Sun Go Down, The Free Press, New York, NY, 2002
Wittgenstein's Lolita and The Iceman, Wild Dog Press, Brush Creek, TN, 2006

SHORT STORY–PUBLICATIONS

'Those Deep Elm Brown's Ferry Blues" *Missouri Review*, (Fall 1998)

"I Hate to See That Evening Sun Go Down" *Georgia Review*, (Fall 1998)

"Closure and Roadkill on the Life's Highway" *Atlantic Monthly*, (November 1999)

"The Paperhanger" *Harpers*, (February 2000)

"A Death in the Woods" *GQ*, (November 2000)

"My Hand Is Just Fine Where It Is" *Oxford American*, (September October 1999)

"The Crimper" *Harpers*, (October 2000)

"Good Til Now" *Oxford American*, (January February 2001)

"Charting the Territories of the Red" *Southern Review* (Spring 2001)

"Wreck on the Highway" *Chattahoochee Review*, (2005)

"Where Will You Go When Your Skin Cannot Contain You?" *Tin House*, (2007)

ARTICLES

"Sweet Songs Never Last Too Long" *Oxford American*, Music Issue, (July August 1999)

"Queen of the Haunted Dell" *Oxford American* (October 2000)

"Sitting on Top of the World" *Oxford American* Music

Issue (2000)

"Time Done Been Won't Be No More" *Oxford American*, (July/August Music Issue, 2001)

"Crossroads Blues" *Oxford American* (2002, website only)

"Blind Willie McTell" *Oxford American*, (Summer, 2005)

"Calves Howling at the Moon" *Oxford American*, (Fall, 2005)

"The Man in the Attic: A Memoir" *Paste*, (June/July, 2006)

"The Banjo Man" *Oxford American*, Music Issue, (Summer, 2006)

ANTHOLOGIES

New Stories from The South, The Year's Best, Edited by Shannon Ravenel, 1998

New Stories from The South, The Year's Best, Edited by Shannon Ravenel, 1999

New Stories from The South, The Year's Best, Edited by Shannon Ravenel, 2000

Best New American Voices, Edited by Tobias Wolff, 2000

New Stories from The South, The Year's Best, Edited by Shannon Ravenel, 2001

O' Henry Prize Stories, Edited by Larry Dark, 2001

Best Mystery Stories, Edited by Lawrence Block, 2001

Best Music Writing, Edited by Nick Hornby, 2001

New Stories from The South: The Year's Best, Edited by Shannon Ravenel, 2002

Stories From the Blue Moon Café, Edited by Sonny Brewer, 2002

Stories from the Blue Moon Cafe II, Edited by Sonny Brewer, 2003

They Write Among Us, Edited by Jim Dees, 2003

Stories from the Blue Moon Cafe III, Edited by Sonny Brewer, 2004

Anchor Book of Modern Short Stories, Edited by Ben Marcus, 2004

Stories from the Blue Moon Cafe IV, Edited by Sonny Brewer, 2004

Best of the South: The Best of the Second Decade, Selected by Anne Tyler, 2005

A Cast of Characters and Other Stories, Edited by Sonny Brewer, 2006

Best American Short Stories, Edited by Steven King, 2007

Best American Mystery Stories, Edited by Carl Hiaasen, 2007

The Surreal South, Edited by Pinckney Benedict, 2007

The Ecco Anthology of Contemporary American Short Fiction, Edited by Joyce Carol Oates and Christopher R. Beha, 2008

The Oxford American Book of Great Music Writing, Edited by Marc Smirnoff, 2008

EDITOR

With Suzanne Kingsbury, *The Alumni Grill, Anthology of Southern Writers,* MacAdam/Cage, 2004.

INTERVIEWS

"Out of Nowhere: After decades of laboring in complete obscurity, Middle Tennessee author William Gay has finally found literary acclaim," by Clay Risen, *Nashville Scene,* (January 16, 2003), p. 23 – 27.

"A Natural Talent: Author William Gay, snug amid woods of his native Hohenwald, reflects on lifelong love of words," by Julie Gillen, *The Daily Herald,* (Sunday, March 7, 2004), 1D, 4D. Columbia, TN.

"An Interview with William Gay," by Georgia Afton, *Water-Stone Review: A Literary Annual*, Volume 7, (Fall 2004), p. 42-59.

Bookmark with Don Noble, "Interview with William Gay," Produced by The Center for Public Television at the University of Alabama (c) 2007 by University of Alabama Center for Public Television (DVD)

"Interview: William Gay," Tennessee Literary Project, MTSU, Conducted by MTSU student Kenny Torrella, (April 13, 2008), www.mtsu.edu/tnlitproj

"Inventing Tennessee's own Yoknapatawpha County," by Clay Risen, (10/2009), Tennessee Committee for the Humanities www.chapter16.org

"William Gay: Featured Writer of the Month," November, 2009, Oxford American web page: www.oxfordamerican.org/interviews/2009/nov/04/feature d-writer-month/

"Positively William Gay," Interviewed by Anthony Scarlati, *Nashville Arts Magazine*, (December 2009), p. 27 - 31.

"Ackerman's Field and Lewis County: Lewis County author William Gay's stories to hit the big screen," by Jordan Blie, *Lewis County Herald*, (January 7, 2010). p. 1, p. 5.

AWARDS

1999 William Peden Award
1999 James A. Michener Memorial Prize
2002 Guggenheim Fellowship
2007 United States Artists Ford Foundation Fellow
2009 Writer of the Year, Tennessee Literary Association

ACKNOWLEDGEMENTS

I'd like to thank William Gay for his generous offer to work with Wild Dog Press to bring out this volume of his collected prose, and for allowing me to photograph his paintings and record our conversations, and finally for the beautiful poetry of his prose. I'd also like to thank Susan McDonald for all her support. Patty Baker, Patti Wagner and Renee Leonard helped with the typing. Lamont Ingalls, a friend and cohort, designed the text, and graphic artist John Cipollina created the cover. Greg Hobson is an amazing photographer whose expertise is much appreciated. Julie Gillen provided her William Gay paintings which were photographed by Mike Gladney. And for their friendship and support of all my endeavors I'd like to thank Susan White, Jerry Risner who helped me find William Gay in Hohenwald, Frank Evans, Anthony Blake, my daughter Coree and my son Coby.

My work on this book is dedicated to the memory of my sister, Betty White Penley, 1934 – 2010.

–jmw

CPSIA information can be obtained at www.ICGtesting.com
Printed in the USA
BVIW12n1114070218
507494BV00008B/89